PENGUIN BOOKS
<u>INSIDE BLACK AUSTR</u>

Kevin Gilbert was born in the small country town of
Condobolin in New South Wales. Directly descended from
Aboriginal, Irish, English stock, he lived in Aboriginal
reserves and fringe settlements until 1957 when he was
sentenced to penal servitude for life on a charge of murder.
He served fourteen and a half years under the New South
Wales prison system. In spite of those tough years he
became the first Aboriginal playwright. His play about
Aboriginal seasonal workers is called *The Cherry Pickers*.
He is a poet, a great talker, an oils artist, and wrote *Because
a White Man'll Never Do it*, the first major political work by
an Aboriginal, and *Living Black*, an Aboriginal oral
history.

Also by Kevin Gilbert
The Cherry Pickers (play)
Because a White Man'll Never Do It
Living Black

INSIDE BLACK AUSTRALIA
AN ANTHOLOGY OF ABORIGINAL POETRY

Edited by Kevin Gilbert

PENGUIN BOOKS

Published with the assistance of the Literature Board of the Australia Council

Penguin Books Australia Ltd
487 Maroondah Highway, PO Box 257
Ringwood, Victoria, 3134, Australia
Penguin Books Ltd
Harmondsworth, Middlesex, England
Viking Penguin Inc.
40 West 23rd Street, New York, NY 10010, USA
Penguin Books Canada Limited
2801 John Street, Markham, Ontario, Canada, L3R 1B4
Penguin Books (N.Z.) Ltd
182–190 Wairau Road, Auckland 10, New Zealand

First published by Penguin Books Australia, 1988

Typeset in Caslon Medium by Abb-typesetting Pty Ltd, Victoria
Made and printed in Australia by Australian Print Group, Maryborough,
Victoria

CIP

Inside Black Australia: an anthology of
Aboriginal poetry.

Includes index.
ISBN 0 14 011126 3.

[1]. Australian poetry – Aboriginal authors.
[2]. Aborigines, Australian – Poetry. 3.
Australia – Poetry. I. Gilbert, Kevin,
1933–

A821'.308089915

Creative writing program assisted by the Literature Board
of the Australia Council, the Federal Government's arts
funding and advisory body.

Dedicated to Aboriginaland

ACKNOWLEDGEMENTS

I gratefully acknowledge the Aboriginal poets for sharing their 'tucker' with us and to those who helped make possible the bringing together of all the material, namely, the Australia Council's Literature Board and Aboriginal Arts Board who in the past supported me with a Writer's Fellowship.

I first sought approval for Kath Walker's (now known as Oodgeroo Noonuccal) and Jack Davis' poems over ten years ago, and have been working consistently on 'finalising' the work for the past three years. This all goes to prove the validity of 'Aboriginal time' as my publisher would hasten to agree.

This book, then, has passed so many deadlines that I was tempted to call it *Lazarus, Lazarus . . .* and only the goodwill and interest of my fellow Black poets kept me on track.

Special acknowledgements also go to Cheryl Buchanan and Lionel Fogarty for permission to reproduce the works of the poets in *Murrie Coo-ee* and other publications of hers. Many thanks also to all the poets whose works were not included in this anthology and to Jackie Yowell and Susan Hawthorne for editorial concern; and last but not least to Elly.

CONTENTS

INTRODUCTION

◄   Over the last two decades the Aboriginal voice has received quite a remarkable amount of attention and scrutiny in the European Australian world of literature. Many, especially those exercising a critical overview and expecting something different, more exotic perhaps, from a people whose traditional expression was an oral tradition, have not come to terms with this often raw, certainly rugged, and definitely truthful subjective material drawn from the creative impulse. There are a number of difficulties in perception and analysis, the most difficult of these is to attempt rationalisation of hundreds of thousands of years of oral tradition against the last twenty years of limited access to white education and education in the alien English tongue.

The successful transformation from oral to written form can be attested by the success of Oodgeroo Noonuccal's (Kath Walker's) writings, Robert Merritt's play, *The Cake Man*, Gerry Bostock's play *Here Comes The Nigger* and the more recent plays of Jack Davis. All of which have won acclaim here and overseas. In 1929 David Unaipon had his *Native Legends* published. This was the first complete work by an Aboriginal. Oodgeroo Noonuccal, with her book of poems *We Are Going*, published in 1964 under her previous name, Kath Walker, became our first poet to be published. Colin Johnson produced the first Aboriginal novel *Wild Cat Falling* in 1965. Jack Davis followed in 1970 with his first published book *The First Born and Other Poems*. In 1973 I completed the first major political work by an Aboriginal *Because A White Man'll Never Do It* and in 1978 *Living Black* the first collection of contemporary Aboriginal oral history from an Aboriginal viewpoint. Altogether 'Aboriginal Writers' as such were very thin on the ground – the merest handful – and, to add to our difficulties, were an unknown market potential.

In the 1980s, with the showing of Hyllus Maris and Sonia Berg's *Women of the Sun* on TV, and of other Aboriginal films, has come the realisation in the Aboriginal community that we can write and express our view more forcibly, and more importantly, more truthfully than can whites writing about or making films about us. The result has been a small avalanche of Aboriginal biographies, plays, political writings and poetry. Many of these writers and poets are fully occupied in producing news magazines and broadsheets within the Aboriginal community, which in turn will ultimately produce a much wider participation in literature within the next decade.

A whole new education 'industry' has arisen in the academic area, where it would appear that every student is doing his or her PhD English thesis on 'Aboriginal Literature'. Some people ask the inevitable questions: What is an Aboriginal poet? How should they be differentiated and why differentiated from any other poet writing in English? Is it necessary to know that they *are* Aboriginal poets provided that the criteria are comparable, i.e. aesthetics, imagery, relationship to traditional forms or drawing on other poetic forms? Aboriginal poetry rattles, flings and bends the chains and rules of verse, sometimes in a remarkable manner. But within each bending one can see the cyclical incantation, the emotional mnemonics, the substance from which Aboriginal poetry is made.

When Europeans see a group of Aboriginals sitting around a camp-fire singing a corroboree song, they say 'corroboree' or 'Blackfellas yackaaing'. But to *understand* what they are doing introduces a whole new area for examination. For instance, most people know what transcendental meditation is about, or yoga positions, or they understand something of the process when some people kneel down, clasp their hands together and look up into the sky, saying, 'Our Father which are in Heaven'. The Aboriginal way is the creative continuum:

At night as I sit by my camp-fire
the Great Serpent Spirit a'star
I sing songs of love to the Presence within
as It plays with the sparks on my fire.*

So, that which is seen as a bit of a sing-a-long, a 'yackaaing' by Blacks, is a deeply sacred and spiritual experience. So much so that, if an uninvited man or woman enters the circle unbidden, they can well court a death sentence, for within that circle the Great Creator Essence is present.

Rarely has Aboriginal poetry much to do with aesthetics or pleasure or the pastoral views, those remarkable views the city person finds in the commonplace torn by bulldozers, overstocking and mining operations. There is another reality, a reality that could find parallels in the experience of the indigenous peoples of South Africa or Bolivia, or of oppressed populations within the national boundaries of one culture, the Jews in Nazi Germany or the Palestinians in Israel. For instance, I was talking to an old man in the desert country, blind from trachoma, one leg lost to leprosy, his hands twisted to a macabre semblance of digitless talons. He sat in the ashes of his camp-fire and, pointing a twig at an equally gnarled and twisted tree, said:

That leaf, the seed, that leaf
my old old grandfather
he was a baby
little fella you know
a big mob camped
a big mob
the horsemen came
guns guns guns
pulled stirrup irons from saddles
bang bang blood
and shit everywhere
his mummy buried him
and 'nother two quick
under rocks and rocks
and her blood run through
the rocks and leaf
the leaf with seed attached
stuck to him
red with seed stuck on
the leaf the leaf
with seed stuck on
the leaf.

In emphasising the leaf, the seed and the rock, the speaker thus assured that I would remember the story thereafter by focussing on the leaf, the rocks, with seed attached to the leaf. In subsequent reiteration, an emotional visual shorthand would be used with the key symbols, selecting the poetic metaphor.

Many critics of Aboriginal poetry, whether using polite language or digital graffiti, express some difficulty in finding comparisons and parallels. Their solemn enunciation on the aesthetics, the imagery, rhyming and metric patterns, metaphors, lucidity, fluidity, lingoism, jingoism, polemicism, chantism, phenomenalism of the Aboriginal voice, is an assurance to us that the debate will long continue. Of course, there will be many who, not wanting to reveal any overt or covert racism, paternalism, condescension, misconception, self-deception or otherwise to the value of the contribution, will dart like a prawn in a barramundi pond to the safety of antecedents. To us it is like seeing a saga of these British Boat People returning to the wreck to salvage a plank and, holding it aloft, try to make comparisons with the indigenous tree and twist it to the semblance of the 'tree back home'.

Aboriginal poets share a universality with all other poets, yet differ somewhat in the traumatic and material experience of other poets, especially those who have wandered through Europe and, for that matter, Australia, starving in ghettos or rejecting established constraints.

Aboriginals have done their starving in mia-mias, gunyahs, shanties or under loose sheets of old iron gathered from the white man's rubbish-tip; in below poverty-level ghettos, or in gaols. For instance, a white South African poet's voice is easily identifiable with his English, Dutch or American counterpart, especially when each so lavishly follows the 'new poetry' trends of the other in the 100th monkey imitation style that was so prevalent in Australia during the 70s. Aboriginal poets, on the other hand, can be identified with the freedom poets of the lately decolonised countries and as a new phenomenon upon the Australian scene, demanding a new perception of life around us, a new relation with the sanctity, the spiritual entity and living Presence within the earth and all life forms throughout the universe.

As Aboriginal bark paintings reveal the fundamental elements of the subject, so too does the Aboriginal poet reveal the fundamental subject of the song. The emotional symbolism is, to a great degree, an extension of the traditional oral language, where the history or song cycle is recorded on bark paintings – symbolic mnemonics which link together the beginning and end of the complex whole – stimulating recall of the intervening detail. In written language we see the poems as emotional mnemonics, which, to fully appreciate their import, one needs to understand a little of the poet, the social and historical context from which is wrought the subjective crystallisation of the voice.

Much of the historical subject of this poetry has been carved indelibly in blood over the past 200 years and before the poets were born. That the psyches still quiver with the shock of these horrendous times can be directly attributed to the continuing brutality, the national lies, the callous indifference to Black human life and the continuing practices of institutionalised racism today.

In an attempt to clarify some of the misconceptions about Aboriginal life and time in this land, I'll draw on some established criteria. The earliest existing record (skeletal remains, carbon dated implements) of the appearance of 'modern man' has been discovered in Australia. Australia has the oldest geological formations in the world and the oldest life forms. Aborigines inhabited this land before the great ice-age, disproving the theory of the land bridge immigration path, in agreement with the Aboriginal story that we have *always* been here.

Aboriginal culture, based on a predictable and unchanging system of Law, obviated any war for possession of land. Each tribal area is the Sovereign Domain of that tribe born into that tribal area, governed by and governing, the social and spiritual system as set down at the Beginning, the start of time. The Dreaming is the first formation, the beginning of the creative process of mobile life/spirit upon and within the land. It is the days of creation when the Great Essence, the Spiritual Entity and minion spirits formed the Aboriginal version of the 'Garden of Eden' and recorded that creation and the laws abounding upon the tjuringas. These laws, this Dreaming, still nurtures the spiritual body of the People who still follow 'the Business' the proper way.

When Captain James Cook landed on these shores he was able

to concede that the Aboriginals wanted for nothing and that their condition, their lot in life was better than that which was available to the European population as a whole. But he was unable to converse or comprehend signs other than those remarkably apparent ones telling him to 'go away' and, seeing that his items of trade held no real or intrinsic value with which he could trick or treat, he declared 'possession' for the Crown, stating that the land was *terra nullius*, wasteland and unoccupied.

The next remarkable episode saw the English soldiers driving Blacks from their Black Sovereign Domain. To legalise the 'dispersion', the soldiers were bidden to call upon the rightful owners, the Blacks, three times in the name of the Crown of England and, if the Blacks did not immediately surrender, to fire upon them. Of course, not understanding English ways nor the English language, the people died in the 'Catch 22' cross-fire. All of which ensured that these representatives of the Crown were very quickly able to kill the rightful owners of the land and claim the spoils as their 'right' by the historical fiction of 'peaceful settlement'.

In my country, Wiradjuri, a large mob of my countrymen, women and children were herded and driven like sheep before the guns to the big swamps near Bathurst. There they were 'dispersed' with guns and clubs, whereupon these pioneering, head-hunting whites cut off a large number of the peoples' heads, boiled them down in buckets and sent 45 of the skulls and other bones off to Britain. In much the same way, they took Pemulwy's head, pickled it and sent it off to the Joseph Banks collection in England. Many people, especially white Australians, who trace their genealogy to the 'First Fleet', are anxious that such gory mementos of the infamous theft of the land and the accompanying inhumanity remain in the colonial closet. While inhumanity continues as it does continue this day in this country, the cry for justice, the cry for humanity will never be silenced.

As I drive towards Queanbeyan on my periodic visits to Canberra, yesterday's crimes wash upon me, wave after wave in the new assault by memory of the old injustice and made more urgent by the new injustices heaped day by day on the contemporary Black community.

On the Way to Queanbeyan

I look at the open fields and see
the space where my people used to be
I see the scars of wounded ground
I cry as I hear the death call sound
of curlew mourning by.

I drive past Mitchell, a suburb of Canberra, and glance towards
the buildings that house some eight hundred Aboriginal skulls,
including many in the Murray Black Collection, taken mostly
from Wiradjuri country, skulls of my ancestors. This triggers my
mind to dwell on many more Aboriginal skeletons lying dis-
respectfully in the State museums around the land, as well as in
many museums overseas; the 'tobacco pouches' made from
dried scrotums of Blacks and used as tobacco pouches; the
bodies skinned for their cicatrice patterns and pickled in the
South Australian Museum basement. I drive along a bit of
bitumen which bears the sign 'This is a Bicentennial Project'. I
pick up the papers and read of 'Black Deaths in Custody', a race
riot in Bourke, where the Government advances the pre-
posterous proposition that what is needed is 'more sporting
facilities'. Perhaps more footballs and tennis rackets to kick their
frustration away, to keep at bay the tyrant killer, white society,
that daily grinds away any hope of justice and a recognised
humanity for Blacks.

I look at the new 'voluntary work for the dole' plan of the
Hawke administration. I know that *his* Government has already
forced Aboriginal communities to work for the dole and called it
community work employment project. I also know that this
scheme caused hardship and increased the level of malnutrition
for Blacks, but it is a sop for the white Australians. It might catch
a few more votes from those right of centre. The fact of this latest
violation of Human Rights passes unnoticed overseas. In the
minds of at least some of my fellow poets is the traumatic image
of yesterday's events, ricocheting into today's boast of peace and
justice and Human Rights' conventions. There is the constant
attempt by white Australia to 'assimilate' Aboriginals; to hold
them politically powerless, by cultural genocide, by stopping
Aboriginal language programmes. To us this is symbolically and

directly representative of another favourite pastime of whites of
yester-year in their sport of 'Lobbing the Distance', which
entailed the burying of live Aboriginal children up to their necks
in sand and seeing who of them could kick off the heads of the
Black children to the farthest distance from its body. Another
pastime in those days, made popular by the close proximity of
good dry firewood, was to cut the throats of Black women and
men and let them run in terrified flapping circles and, when they
collapsed, throw the bodies while still alive upon the fire. Live
children where thrown directly into the flames.

Moving to less grim moments in Black history, the Aboriginals
were finally chained and exiled in areas euphemistically called
'reserves'. Here they were kept under the control of police and
camp commandants or under the hardly less barbaric control of
the missionaries. Apartheid laws were enacted and co-habiting
with whites *in loving relationship* was savagely punished, while
house slavery and sexual abuse was considered more or less a
'civilising' influence. Slavery was called 'wardship'. Pass-laws
and curfews such as not being near any town *after* sunset, on the
pain of imprisonment or death, left a lot to be said for our so
called civilised invaders.

The missionaries, full of savage zeal to 'convert' the heathen
also wanted to stake a claim to title upon Aboriginal land, much
of which they still hold onto, topping up their coffers from time
to time by selling off a bit of the ill-gotten real estate. The
missionaries aided the attempt to destroy the Aboriginal culture
by kidnapping and imprisoning young Blacks and placing them in
separate male and female compounds (concentration camps),
where they were kept estranged from their tribal family until
they were in their late teens. The children were not allowed to
speak Aboriginal language in many of these 'missions' and were
discouraged by the simple expedient of locking an offender away
in solitary confinement on a bread and water diet, often for as
long as twenty-one days. If they repeated the offence, their hair
was cut off, they were 'chastised' and again put in isolation. If a
girl waved her hand at a boy who passed her compound fence,
her ways were curbed by cutting off her hair, a few chops with the
cane and several weeks in solitary to 'cool off'. Of course this
meant her saying, 'Hello' in the lingo was a punishable offence.

For many of us the missionary zeal has meant the loss of our traditional tongue, the more quickly to heed and comprehend the dreamed of commands that would be delivered by 'the master' to us in the role of tinker, tailor, drover, Jacky, dishwasher, maid and cane-cutter as he, in his wild erratic fancy, imagined our destined roles to be.

These memories, these experiences, are juxtaposed in the twentieth century for the majority of Aboriginals with the sub-human conditions they are still living under: many are denied access to rivers and waterholes by pastoralists and miners; living in confined areas where they can no longer move camp and hunt; living permanently under scraps of tarpaulin and hessian and derelict car bodies; dying in custody at the hands of the 'enforcers of the law'; dying from curable eighteenth century diseases; blinded by trachoma; dying from malnutrition and dying in droves from Hepatitis B because the Gubba'ment won't provide the cost for the immunisation – $150 per person – so they die without a murmur of protest, except that of the thundering roar of outrage by the Flying Doctor Service, whom the whites have chosen to ignore because they feel that someone like the Flying Doctor Service should only comment upon and tend whites in the outback. This 'blind spot' in the racist's eye causes the Aboriginal to suffer one of the highest infant mortality rates in the world. Life expectancy for adult males is but forty-nine years, while a Black woman's life expectancy is a mere fifty-two years; some twenty years less than that of whites whose culture has successfully been cloned from the English one and become a parasite on Aboriginal land and resources.

As I write this introductory piece, as other poets write more poems, more people die. In Australia, Blacks die needlessly, shamefully, and their death can be contributed directly to a lie: the lie Captain James Cook gave birth to when he declared this land *terra nullius*, a wasteland and unoccupied. In so doing, he lied away Aboriginal life, proprietary right and therefore right of Sovereign Domain to our rightful land and gave every murderer, every rapist, every thief, every sadist, every racist an open pass to kill, torture, enslave and take at will everything that had been protected, nurtured, sanctified and kept spiritually intact from the Dreaming.

How many will remember *Aboriginal* history as Australia marches to the 1988 Bicentenary to celebrate the *terra nullius* fiction – the lie of peaceful settlement – while Aboriginals and people from all round the world see the celebration of thieves holding the garment aloft, the spoils of theft and mass murder? How many poets shall sing? Black poets sing, not in odes to Euripides or Dionysus, not Keats, nor Browning, nor Shakespeare; neither do they sing a pastoral lay to a 'sunburnt country' for they know that that russet stain that Dorothea Mackellar spoke of is actually the stain of blood, our blood, covering the surface of our land so the white man could steal our land.

These poems, these voices are unforgettable and remain emotionally intact long after the words have passed from memory. It is the echo of the sea crooning inside a sea-shell many leagues away from the seashore, the quick drawn breath of a woman who comes suddenly upon an image, a face, a scene that reminds her of a loved one; a song once sung and now only memory orchestrates for one brief moment the emotion, the flash of sweetness and the pain. The pain. These poems then are not poems of protest, but rather, poems of life, of reality. The poetry of a people concerned with life and loving and dignity and justice, birth, regeneration and children and the land and they are saying how, where and why. *Why* has it gone so wrong?

Kevin Gilbert

W. LES RUSSELL

◄   W. Les Russell, Boolidt Boolidtha, was born in Melbourne, 1949. Les spent his early years in rural Victoria. He joined the Royal Australian Navy in 1965, and trained as a photographer in the Fleet Air Arm. However, his upbringing and beliefs were not compatible with the servile martial-anglo-christian ethics of the Navy so he requested and was granted an honourable discharge in 1970. For the following ten years, he worked as a photographer for the Education Department of Victoria. In between poems, he helped set up the South Eastern Land Council and later served on that body as chairman. His dedication and hard word in the Black community gained wide respect which, in turn, meant an extraordinary workload and responsibility, especially in his home state of Victoria. He served as Honorary Cultural Officer with Aboriginal Education; was co-founder of the Mara Organisation, which assisted in the struggle at Portland against Alcoa; worked with the Aboriginal Advancement League on the Government's proposed changes to the Archaeological Act; helped set up a mock oil rig on the grounds of St Paul's Cathedral, Melbourne, to raise awareness and support for the people of Noonkanbah, and so the list could go on. In 1979 he was asked to help the North Queensland Land Council set up and chair the Aboriginal Mining Information Centre. He helped make this organisation one of the largest indigenous research bodies in the world, with capabilities to monitor the plans and behaviour of those who pose as 'developers' of this country.

In 1986, Les' poems were printed in *Greed For Green*, published by Impact Media Productions. His poem 'Tali Karng: Twilight Snake', first printed in *This Australia* magazine, Winter 1985 (Vol. 4 no. 3), shows a control and imagery far beyond the parameters of the majority of Australian poets to that greater universal level beyond country, beyond life.

◄ # Tali Karng: Twilight Snake

Tali Karng: twilight snake:
In the crater lies the lake.
Water tan; deep'n dark;
Cold lake bed of leaves and bark.
Rugged steep crater wall
Covered o'er in grey-green tall
Alpine and Mountain Ash
Where dainty birds cavort and flash;
Branch to branch, and sweetly sing
Till sudden comes the gold evening,
And;
Tali Karng: twilight snake:
Hunts near waters of the lake.

▪

◄ # Red

Red is the colour
of my Blood;
of the earth,
of which I am a part;
of the sun as it rises, or sets,
of which I am a part;
of the blood
of the animals,
of which I am a part;
of the flowers, like the waratah,
of the twining pea,
of which I am a part;
of the blood of the tree
of which I am a part.
For all things are a part of me,
and I am a part of them.

▪

◄ Ngarnbarndtar

Ngarnbarndtar
dytimbiarngka ngearmboom ngailala ningkai?
Dtakkarndtibee?
Ngarnbarndtar
dtyimbiarngka ngearmboom ngailala ningkai?
Dtakkarndtibee?
Ngarnbarndtar
dytimbiarngka ngearmboom ngailala ningkai?
Dtakkarndtibee?

(Who is that
sitting this side of my fire?
Is it a Spirit that brings sickness?)

(A rude person who doesn't know the laws,
is encroaching within the Land of which
I am a part: coveting, stealing.)
■

◄ The 'Developers'

Like a spear thrust deep within my heart
the drill turns deep within the earth.
Like the Yulo makes the soul depart
the Company kills with greedy mirth.

Like with a shield to parry blows
I now use words and demonstrate
against all wrong that I know,
I will not assimilate.

I am this Land and it is mine,
I cannot change and to it be true.
I cannot let the Company mine,
I cannot give this Land to you.

When you can learn to respect the Land,
when you can live within her.
When you can, with pride, stand
and say you understand her,

I'll still not give, it's not my right,
what man can give his Mother;
but I'll proudly share with all my might
and call you my own brother.

■

◄ God Gave Us Trees to Cut Down

My Goodness;
if I was to have a say in the way things should be done in
    Victoria:
like we run them and have them here in Queensland,
then by crikey;
those forests – rainforests and what have they – in Gippsland
    there;
and let me tell you,
we have been down this road with the conservationists too:
and, by golly, we gave them what for.

And why should they cut down their trees?
What use are they? well I'll tell you:
the Japanese – I know they're a funny mob of people –
but they make paper out of trees, see,
and we all need paper.
You know this – what a stupid question to ask.
What would you do without paper and cardboard and –
    goodness, I ask you.
Of course we must cut down trees;
golly, what did God give them to us for.

And look at the other States, and all of them and what have
    you;
they have taken a leaf out of our Queensland way of doing
    things.
Just look at Mr Grey in Tasmania; he cuts down many trees,
now; unfortunately they don't seem to have the courage
to stand up to the Federal Government and sit firmly on their
    position
– but let me tell you, they cut down many trees in Tasmania.
And in Western Australia
– just look at them – well –
they cut down their Jarra, and all their other sorts there.
And in New South Wales previous governments,
and even the present government sells their trees to the
    Japanese,

and my goodness, so they should.
Don't worry about South Australia, they don't have any trees.
Unfortunately the Northern Territory has been given to the
    Aboriginals,
and we all know they worship trees and sticks and plants and
    things
and what have you
and all sorts of things so we all know where that place is
    going;
and what a pity:
minerals and the Casino and Ayers Rock
– as they now call it: Uluru; and what a shame – don't you
    think it a shame?
And you see? they worship rocks too. All the minerals will go
    down the drain.

But here in Queensland we don't let the Federal Government
down there in Canberra tell us what to do
– and why should we?
If they come up here we soon give them short shrift and short
     change.
We send them running back down south with their tails
     between their legs
and their hats behind their backs like little school boys.
That's the way to do it – you've got to show them who's boss.
And so I would tell Mr Cain not to worry about those
     conservationists,
just run right over them:
cut right through the lot of them as if they weren't there.
Golly, that's the way we do it in Queensland.

My goodness, you should know
God gave us those rainforests to cut down...

Poet's note: Anyone acquainted with Queensland politics will
recognise the voice in this poem.

■

◄ # The Nuclear Winter

*Dedicated to Djilby, my Brother:
a Victim of Nuclear Testing.*

Lying in a cold hell,
It's dark, but she's blind;
Dying in her own cell,
No food left to find,

because:

The agony of Nuclear,
The land turned to glass,
Then came long night, cold drear,
And years bitter pass.

The Nuclear winter.

No future but slow cruel death
Bequeathed by those whose seed
Brought forth life and breath
To her, and this mad deed.
This tiny waif dying there;
Crying there
Alone.   Alone!

Play the games Nuclear,
Only our children need fear.
    Who is that dying there?
       Who is that crying there?
   Is she your grandchild dear?
There on her own.

▪

LAJAMANU POETS

◄ Literacy Teachers from the Northern Territory share their poems with us in the Language and translate into English.

Pansy Rose Napaljarri is 22 years old, has one son and works at the Lajamanu School, Hooker Creek, in the Northern Territory, where she translates into her native language: Warlpiri.

Rhonda Samuel Napurrurla is 22 years old, translates English into Warlpiri. Rhonda collects Legends from the Old People, and types the stories into the computer to make books for the children.

Irene James Napurrurla is 26 years old. She makes small reader books for children in the grade 2–3–4– level, and says; 'It is good to teach our own children to read in our own language because we don't want our language to die.'

Julie Watson Nungarrayi has two sons, comes from Lajamanu, and, with

Valerie Patterson Napanangka also of Lajamanu, reads the Warlpiri books to the children in class.

Jennie Hargraves Nampijinpa, very much aware of the traps and tribulations of media technology, nevertheless loves the interest and excitement of languages and computers.

PANSY ROSE NAPALJARRI

◄ Marlu-Kurlu

Ngapa, kanunju pamarrpa-wana,
karlimi ka pulya-nyayirni, karru-jangka
pamarrpa-kurra.
Jurlpu-patu kalu nyinami watiya witangka,
jinjirla kalu parntinyanyi kuja kalu pardimi yalyu-yalyu.

Marlu ka ngunami yamangka,
mata-nyayirni parnkanja-warnu.
Ngapa ka purdanyanyi,
kuja ka pulya karlimi.

Wardinyi ka nguna, yapa-wangurla luwarninja-kujaku,
jinjirla ka parntinyanyi,
matalku ka jarda-jarrimi.
■

◄ The Kangaroo

Water beneath the hills,
running slowly from the creek,
towards the hills.

Birds sitting on the branch,
smelling the red flowers
that are growing.

Kangaroo is lying in the shade,
very tired from hopping around,
he listens to the water,
that is running very slowly.

He is happy, no people around,
to spear him.
He smells the red flowers,
so tired, he goes to sleep.

■

◄ Muturna-Jarra-Kurlu Kujalpa-Pala
Wangkaja

Yamangka kapala ngatinyanu-jarra nyina wanta-kujaku.
Kuja-kapala nyinami, wangkami-kapala-nyanu yapa-patu-kurlu.
Nakamarraju ka kuja-nganta wangkami Nampijinpa-kuju,
'Yuwa,
nyangunpa-jana ngula wati-patu kujalpalu rarralykajirla
kilji-nyayirni warru yanu?' Nampijinpa-ju-rla yalumanu,
'Yuwayi, manu kuja kalu tarnngajiki warru parnkami
rarralykajirla-juku, wapanja-wangu. Kala yangka ngalipa
kuja kalarlipa tarnnga-parnta wapaja nyurruwiyi.
Wankaru-ku-wiyi-rli-jana ngatinyanurlu manu kurdanyanurlu
wankirri mani, ngularra-ku ngayi wati-patu-ku, kuja kalu
tarnnga-parntarlu waru kanyi rarralykaji'.

Nakamarra-julpa-nyanu wangkaja kuja, 'Ngularra-rlangu
karnta-karnta kuja kalu warrarda yani wati-patu-kurlu,
yangka kuja kalu-nyanu kalinja palka mardarni.
Mimayirli-jiki-rli-nyanu pakarnirra, pakarnirra kaji yapa
jinta wapamirra yalyu-wangu. Ngula karnta-karnta, kulalpalu
wati jinta-kurlu nylnayarla, walku'.

Nampijinpa-jurla Nakamarra-kuju wangkaja, 'Manu yangka
kuja
kalu pama-kurra warrarda parnkami. Pama-wangu-rlangulu
nyina. Kujangku-juku kapurlu-nyanu kulu-ku, kulu-ku mani,
warlalja-jarra-rlangurlu. Kapulu-nyanu tarnnga-kurra
pakarni'.

Nakamarraju waŋkaja, 'Karnta-karnta-rlaŋu kulalpalu
kurdiji-kirra yantarlarni, walku. Parlpirrpa-rlajuku
yuŋulu parntarrimi, wirntinja-waŋu. Yii . . .
punku-wati-nyayirni, ŋurrpa kapulu kujajiki nyina'.

Ŋulajaŋkaju Nampijinpaju karrinja-pardija manu
Nakamarra-ku-rla waŋkaja, 'Yani karna ŋurra-kurralku.
Ŋakarnaŋku nyanyi jukurrarlu'. Nampijinpaju
ŋurra-kurralku yanu waŋkanja-warnuju.

■

◄ Two women sit in the shade away from the hot sun

Two women sit in the shade away from the hot sun. As they
sit, they discuss the behaviour of others in their community.
Nakamarra says to Nampijinpa,
'Did you see the way those young men drive around so fast in
their car?'

Nampijinpa replies,
'Yes! They never walk around, not like before when we used
to walk everywhere. For their own sakes, their parents should
tell them off not to speed around like that.'

Nakamarra reflected,
'And those girls who go out with the men all the time. You
know, those men who are already married. If they have a fight
over a man, let them fight till one woman walks out without
being hurt. Those girls, they never stay honest to their
husbands, no!'

To Nakamarra, Nampijinpa says,
'And those men who always go out to drink grog. Why don't
they stay off the grog? That's why they fight a lot when they
get drunk. They even fight with their own relation. They
might kill each other.

Nakamarra says,
'And those women should come to corroboree instead of
bending their backs playing cards. They should dance
whenever there is a corroboree. Oh . . . it is so dreadful they
should be so ignorant!'

Nampijinpa stands saying to Nakamarra,
'I am going home. I will see you tomorrow.'

Nampijinpa goes to her own camp.
■

RHONDA SAMUEL NAPURRURLA

◄ Ngati-Nyanu-Jarra-Kurlu

Nyinami kapala warlu-wana wuraji-wurajirla ngati-nyanu-jarra wangkami-kapala yuntalpa-kurlu. Jinta-kariji Napangardi manu jinta-kariji Nangala.

Rdijurnu Nangala-ju wangkanjaku wangkajalpa
    nyanungu-nyangu
yuntalpa-kurlu kujaka warrarda yanirni kutu-karirla pitiyawu-jangka. Kuja-kulalpa Nangalaju wangkaja 'Ngaju-nyangu Napaljarri-ji ka warrarda yani kutu-karirla pitiyawu-jangka?'

Nyarrpararla-mayi kalu nyanyi yartuwajiji mirni-marda kalumpari yuwarli-patu-wana?'
'Paniya-jarrarluju kalu murru-murru-wangurlu mayi kalu nyanyi manu pala-pala-wangurlu?'

Napangardilki-pa wangkaja 'Wara nyiya-wiyi ngaju-nyanguju yuntalpaju waya jukuka purda-nyanyi ngulaju mirntangali-jangka manu wuraji-wuraji-kurra. Walku-nyayirni junga-kalaka purdanyanyi, purdanyanyi, purdanyanyi tarnngangu-juku kapurnarla linpa-wangkami-wiyi Nangala-kuju?

'Kajinpa purdanyanyi ngula waya tarnngangu manu kilji-nyayirnirli kapurnpa warungkalku nyinami?' Kuja kularla wangkaja Napangardiji Nangala-kuju.

■

◄ The Two Mothers

The two mothers both sit down near the fire at evening
talking about their daughters.
The one is Napangardi and the other is Nangala.

The Nangala started to say a few words about her daughter.
She said, 'My daughter Napaljarri always comes after
midnight from watching videos.
I don't even know where she watches videos, maybe
somewhere in those houses.
Her two eyes don't even hurt and she doesn't even get cramp
from watching the video.'

Then later the other woman Napangardi started to say a few
words about her daughter too.
'Oh no wait till you hear about my daughter Nangala. She
keeps listening to the radio, she listens to the radio from 8.30
in the morning until to 7.30 in the night!

'She keeps listening, listening, true. She never stops listening
to the radio. I think I better put a stop to her. I said "when
you listen to the radio so aloud, you will go deaf." That's
what I said to my daughter Nangala.'

■

IRENE JAMES NAPURRURLA

◄ Ngapa-Kurlu

Ngapajilpa parnkaja pirli-wana wita-wana manu
wiri-wana.
Jurlpujulpa wangkaja watiyarla manu
kuyu-watilpalu wapaja
wardapi manu yankirri manu nyiya-kanti-kanti.

Mangkurdulpalu turnu-jarrija,
mayawunparlulpa kujurnu watiya manu marna
wurnturu-nyayirni.

Ngulajangkaju yapa-patulu yanu wirlinyi.
Walku nyangurlurla kuyuku nyiya-kanti-kantiki.

Nyarrpararlalu kuyu-wati muku yanu?

Jurlpulpalu paar-pardija.
nyiya-kanti-kanti
yukuri yalyu-yalyu manu yurrpurlu
walya-ngurlu.

Wantajulpa yukajarra pirli wiri-wana
yalyu-yalyu-nyayirni.

Mungangkalkulpalu jurlpu-wati jardaju
ngunaja watiyarla minangka
manu kuyu nyiya-kanti-kantilpalu muku
ngunaja walyangka.

Yapaju kalu yani pina ngurra-kurra
kuyu-wangu manu yingka-wangu.
Wiyarrpa kalu yani yapa-patuju
wiyarrpa!

■

◄ The Water

Water running past the rocks, small rocks and big rocks.
Birds talking in the trees and animals walking – goanna, emu
and many other animals.

Clouds gathering big wind blowing, throwing trees and grass,
so far away.

Then men came hunting saw nothing of any kinds of animal.
'Where are all the animals gone?'

Birds fly away, birds of many colours, green, red, black
away from the ground.

The sun setting down behind the hill so red, the night came,
birds sleeping in their nest, and animals of all kinds sleeping
on the ground.

The men go home without any food and so sad, without
laughter.
Poor men! SORRY!
■

VALERIE PATTERSON
NAPANANGKA

◄ Ngapa-Kurlu

Ngapa ka wantimi
wantimi ka nyiyaku, nyiya kanti-kantiki
watiyaku, jinjirlaku, yukaku, manu ngarninjaku
watiya yungurlu pardimi, jinjirla yungurlu pardimi
yuka yungurlu pardimi, manu ngapa yungurlipa ngarni
ngurrju-nyayirni kujaka ngapa wantimi.
■

◄ The Rain

It's raining,
what does it rain for? For everything,
for trees, flowers, grass and to drink out in the bush.
So that trees can grow, flowers can grow and so people can
    drink it.
'Oh', it's so good when it rains.
■

◄ Nantuwu-Kurlu

Nantuwu ka parnkami
parnkami ka wukarra
wukarra ka parnkami kurdu-kurdu-kujaku
wajirli-pinyi kalu watiya-kurlurlu manu pamarrpa-kurlurlu
wiyarrpa nantuwu nyurnu manu wijini-kirli
walku, wajampa-wangurlu kalu wajirli-pinyi
parra-kari parra-kari kujajuka
wiyarrpa nantuwu wajampa mani kaju ngajuju.
■

◄ The Horse

A horse is running,
running scared,
running away from kids,
chasing it with sticks and stones.
Poor horse, sick with sores,
chasing it without feeling sorry for it.
Day by day, it just goes on,
poor horse, it makes me feel sad.

■

JULIE WATSON NUNGARRAYI

◄ Yapa Kujalpalu Nyinaja Nyurruwiyi

Yukajarna pirnkingka kaninjarni
witangka pirnkingka kanunju mungapiyarla.
Manulparna warru nyangu pirli kujalpa waraly-waraly-karrija

kaninjarra-kari kartirdi-piya-kurlu
kulanganta kapi-ngalpa pajirni.

Kujarna ngunaja kankalarra-kari
wurnpa-nyayirni pirnkiji nyinanjakuju.

Marlu jurlpungu kankalarra
manu warna yanu

wardapi parnkaja manu yankirri yanu.

Manngulparnaju wangkaja ngajuku nganangku nyampuju
    yirrarnu;
yalyu-yalyu, maru-maru, walya-walya manu kardirri
nganangku mayi yirrarnu nyampuju?

Nyurruwiyilpalu yirrarnu yapangku ngalipa wangurla
manu kajana marlaja ngunami kuruwarri nyurruwarnu.

Walku nyinaja-jana yapaku manu mardukujalu
kujalpalurla karlaja yangun}unguku
ngulaju walku jarrijalu nyurruwiyi.

Manu kajana marlaja ngunami kuruwarri mipa
kujalpalu yirrarnu pirnkingka kaninjarni nyurruwiyi
nyiya-kanti-kanti kirli.

■

◄ Sorry

I crawled in.
It was low and dark.
The rocks hung down like teeth.
Teeth that tried to bite.
Teeth that tried to keep the paintings safe.

I lay on my back.
It was too low to sit up.
Marlu jumped across the roof,
Snakes slithered,
Goanna ran,
Emu strutted.

I thought who put these here?
Who painted them with brush of chewn stick,
Some red, some white, some brown, some black?
Long ago they put them here . . .
Those old Nyiyapali men.
Long ago, now this is all that's left.

Gone are those proud hunters, the women digging mata.
Their language, their dance and song.
All that is left of a people now
Tiny painted animals.

SORRY!
■

JENNIE HARGRAVES NAMPIJINPA

◄ Yuntalpa-Ku

Kurdu yampiya waya
manu pitiyawu kapanku
paniya ngawu-mani
nyanjarla-nyanjarla.

Waya-rlangu manyu-karriya
pulya-karri-karri
kapunpa langa rdulpardimi!

Yampiya kunjuru kaji kanpa papimi
manu jinta-kariji
pama-rlangu yampiya!
Kapunpa-nyanu jalpingki pirlirrpa-pinyi.
Ngurrju-nyinaya.

Yampiya kardiya-kurlangu
waya pama kunjuru pitiyawu
manu nyiya-kanti-kantiji!

Yantarni yawulyu-kurra manu purlapa-kurra
yantarni wirlinyi-kirra manu wirntinja-ku
yantarni kajinpa nyuntu-nyangu warlalja kuruwarri
milya-pinyi.

■

◄ Child, leave the tape recorder

Child, leave the tape recorder
and video alone. It will make
your eyes go very sore if you
look and look at it all the time.

Play the music a bit low,
or else, your ears will explode
from listening to it.

Leave cigarettes alone or they
might burn you and another thing
is, leave the grog alone too.
You might make yourself sick.
Be good!

Leave the White man's things
music, grog, cigarettes, video
and those other things as well!

Come to the ceremonies
come hunting and dancing,
come, so that you can know your
own culture.

■

EVA JOHNSON

◄   Eva Johnson was born at Daly River, Northern Territory. Eva was forcibly taken away from her mother by white authorities when she was three years old, and brought up on Croker Island Mission.

She moved to Adelaide in 1957, went through her school years and became interested in theatre in 1979, joining Black Theatre for their first performance at the Union Hall, Adelaide, in *When I Die, You'll all Stop Laughing*. Since then she has acted in Troupes' production of *Samizdat*, the TV series *Women of the Sun*, Black Theatre's *Onward To Glory*. She wrote and co-directed the play *Tjindarella*. She gained wide acclaim at the Aboriginal Playwrights' Conference in Canberra, 1987 for her play *Murras*, the story of a mother's spiritual power.

Eva is currently a full-time student studying for a Bachelor of Arts Degree, majoring in Drama, as well as writing her book, a biographical history, *In Search of My Mother's Dreaming*.

Eva draws upon her experience of life and knowledge of the Black community. She wrote to a friend, 'I write about some of the special people whom I love, people who are important to us, and who are victims of an inhumane environment.'

◄ Right To Be

Don't stereotype an image of what you want me to be
I'm a Woman and I'm Black and I need to be free
I'll give back your sense of values you bestowed upon me
And regain my pride, my culture, and true identity.

To the future I will strive and there's no looking back
I'll look to other women to support me on my track
I'll fight as a Woman for the right just to be
The most important contribution to this society.

Yes, I'm a Woman and I know that there's nothing that I lack
I'll progress with my learning till I finally get the knack
It's my independent thinking that makes me feel so strong
Our trust in solidarity, simply means we can't go wrong.

I don't want to be no second hand rose
I don't want to be on your centrefold pose
I'm a Woman and I'm Black and I need to be free
Being upfront and powerful is the only way to be.

■

◄ A Letter To My Mother

I not see you long time now, I not see you long time now
White fulla bin take me from you, I don't know why
Give me to Missionary to be God's child.
Give me new language, give me new name
All time I cry, they say – 'that shame'
I go to city down south, real cold
I forget all them stories, my Mother you told
Gone is my spirit, my dreaming, my name
Gone to these people, our country to claim
They gave me white mother, she give me new name
All time I cry, she say – 'that shame'
I not see you long time now, I not see you long time now.

I grow as Woman now, not Piccaninny no more
I need you to teach me your wisdom, your lore
I am your Spirit, I'll stay alive
But in white fulla way, you won't survive
I'll fight for Your land, for your Sacred sites
To sing and to dance with the Brolga in flight
To continue to live in your own tradition
A culture for me was replaced by a mission
I not see you long time now, I not see you long time now.

One day your dancing, your dreaming, your song
Will take me your Spirit back where I belong
My Mother, the earth, the land – I demand
Protection from aliens who rule, who command
For they do not know where our dreaming began
Our destiny lies in the laws of White Man
Two Women we stand, our story untold
But now as our spiritual bondage unfold
We will silence this Burden, this longing, this pain
When I hear you my Mother give me my Name
I not see you long time now, I not see you long time now.

■

◄ Remember?

Born by river
Gently rested on a lily pad
Woman – tired eyes
Wading beside filling string bag with lily roots,
    fish, small tortoise, buds
Woman – singing

Around fire, night time sitting
With Kin – sharing food
        cooked in hot ashes
Children laughing,
        Mother singing
    baby on breast
Women telling stories, sharing, giving
Songs, spirit names, teaching
    IN LANGUAGE.

No more river – Big dam now
String bag empty
       Supermarket now
Women sitting in big houses
         sharing, singing, remembering
         Mother crying, baby clinging
Women telling stories,
       new stories, new names
         NEW LANGUAGE . . .

■

◀ Weevilly Porridge

Weevilly porridge I'm going insane
Weevilly porridge gonna wreck my brain
Stir in treacle, make'em taste sweet
Put'em on stove, turn'em up heat
Milk from powder tin, milk from goat
Weevilly porridge, pour'em down throat.

MmmMmm, mission food, send'em from heaben must be good
MmmMmm, mission food, send'em from heaben must be good

Nebba mind the weevil, nebba mind the taste
Missionary she bin say, 'don't you waste'
Weevilly porridge make'em pretty strong
Spread'em on Dampa can't go wrong.

Bless'em little weevil, bless'em little me
We bin lunga trick'em just you see
Catch'em little weevil, put'em in the tea
Only fullah drink'em up Missionary.

Protector He bin call on us give us daily ration
Cook'em plenty food for Him, together we bin mash'em
Weevils in the sago, weevils in the rice
Protector He bin lunga saying – Mmmm, taste nice.

■

MARY DUROUX

Mary Duroux lives in Kempsey, New South Wales where, for many years, she has worked with various Aboriginal services and cultural committees, mostly in an executive role. Her latest position is with the Central Coast Regional Aboriginal Land Council.

Mary is of a mature age, and of the Thungutti. She is a fine artist as well as a sensitive, lyrical poet.

Mary Duroux has had her few poems included in a wide range of community journals and one day, hopefully, we will see her produce a volume of them for the many fans who have long awaited a book of her poems.

◄ Dirge for a Hidden Art

The legendary life of a long-ago tribe
    Is told on the wall of a cave.
Where grass has grown on the corroboree ground
    And the totem lies in its grave.
How the ashes were scattered by wind and rain
    And the gunyahs have rotted away,
When the tribe of the Yuin departed this land
    And memories were left to decay.

No one can remember the tales that were told
    Of their culture, dreamtime and lore.
The warriors so brave with the weapons they made
    Have died in the days of yore.
Now I'm an old man and the last of my tribe
    And I'm lonely as a human can be
I weep silent tears as I trace each line
    For these pictures were painted by me.

■

◄ Lament for a Dialect

Dyirringan is lost to the tribes of the Yuin,
　　I am filled with remorse and I weep at the ruin
O beautiful words that were softly spoken,
　　Now lay in the past, all shattered and broken,
We forgot it somehow when English began,
　　The sweet sounding dialect of Dyirringan.
If we're to be civilised whom can we blame,
　　To have lost you, my language, is my greatest shame.

■

ERNIE DINGO

◄ Ernie Dingo is one of our best Black stage and film actors on the circuit today. His poetry, like that of his cousin, poet Charmaine Paper-Talk Green, shows the depth of his involvement with grass-roots home country.

On stage, his traditional dancing transports the audience from the footwalk and four walls of the enclosing stage back into the spinifex, gum-tree and campfire magic of our cultural heartland.

With his ability, it is easy to see why so many of the movies and stage-plays in which he has acted have won national and international acclaim. He has appeared in Middar Aboriginal Theatre, (Dance), and in many plays by Jack Davis including *Dreamers*, *Kullark* and *No Sugar*. He also appeared in a film directed by Phil Noyce, and he performed at the First National Aboriginal Playwrights Conference held in Canberra in 1987.

◄ The tracks and the traces
Are all that's behind,
Yet I still see the people
In the back of my mind.
■.

◄ Aboriginal achievement
Is like the dark side of the moon,
For it is there
But so little is known.
■

◄ We are not
Strangers
In our own country
Just
Strangers
To a European society
And it is hard
To be one
When
The law
Is the other.

■

BOBBI SYKES

◄   Bobbi Sykes was born in 1945 in Townsville, Queensland.
She completed her Masters Degree at Harvard University,
Graduate School of Education in 1980 and received her
Doctorate Degree also from Harvard University in 1983 with a
dissertation on *Incentive, Achievement and Community: An
Analysis of Black Viewpoints On Issues Relating to Black
Australian Education* (in press). Her other works include: *Love
Poems and Other Revolutionary Actions*, Saturday Centre,
Sydney, 1979; *Mum Shirl*, Heinemann Publishers, Melbourne,
1981; 'Black Women and the Women's Movement' in *Women
Who Do and Women Who Don't*, Robyn Rowland (Ed.),
Routledge and Kegan Paul Publishers, London, 1984.

    She was the winner of the Peter B. Livingstone Fellowship
Award at the Harvard School of Medicine, Department of
Psychiatry, for her work in power relationships analysis, and the
winner of the Patricia Weickhardt – Black Writers Award (1982),
Victorian Fellowship of Australian Writers.

    Mother of two children, Bobbi is an Executive Member of
Black Women's Action, an organisation which has Black females
and Black males as members. Her current position is a Fellow at
the Centre for Studies in Justice at Mitchell College, Sydney.

    Bobbi's poetry has been widely acclaimed and printed in
books and journals including *Australian Women Poets*, edited
by Susan Hampton and Kate Llewellyn, Penguin Books, Melbourne, 1986, and has had a far reaching and stimulating effect
for other young Aboriginal poets.

    In the long gone days of her participation in the Gurindji
Campaign, Ningla Ana, Black Rights Committees, Black Medical
and Legal Service formation period, and as an active campaigner
at the Aboriginal Tent Embassy in Canberra in 1972 and
outspoken advocate within Australia and overseas for Land
Rights for Blacks, Human Rights and Women's Rights, Dr. Bobbi
Sykes has earned and deserves that special spot in a people's
history reserved for a Black patriot. In her own words then, she
says, 'My poetry *is* my biography'.

◄ Prayer to the Spirit of the New Year

Dear Spirit,
Here we are – at the end of a long year of struggle
Against foes of old – oppression, hunger, pain,
And we stand again at the threshold of a New Year . . .

Let this be a year not just of the same,
Let me not hear again the cry of anguish
From the gaol –

Let me not hear again the sounds of mourning
From young parents . . . of younger infants.

Let me not hear again the crunch
of Baton on bare flesh and bone
And let me not hear again   the silence.

Let me not see the un-cried tears
Welling in the eyes of my black sisters
As they perceive even the little dream they had
Die.

And
Let me not see the veiled defeat
Behind eyes drugged into dreamtime
In the strained faces of my brothers.

And instead
If I might see the slow dawning *begin*
the dawn of understanding

the slow opening
of eyes and hearts *begin*

the slow death
of hypocrisy *begin*

the slow end
of racism *begin*

For legend tells us, dear Spirit,
that in the beginning . . .
■

◄ Requiem

Neatly pressed / dressed / crowds /
Lined up to wave / flags / and babes /
    At the Queen /

I could see first / your stony eye /
And I knew you weren't here /
    To welcome /

But to reject / the 8th descendant /
Of George the Third / in whose name /
    Years ago /

Our land was claimed for Him / now Her /

And you were magnificent / straight as die /
Let them know that this /
Was no country of beaten losers /
But proud warriors /
        Whose time has almost come
■

◄ Fallin'

The Sister has been raped, they said.

I squeezed my eyes tight-shut – in horror,
though I knew, knew, knew, that the horror had just begun;
In shock, but not in disbelief, I heard,
      by five Brothers.

And I thought
Brother, flesh of my flesh,
You have watched / while we / your sisters
cried, gave birth, died, went insane, tore out our own hair,
spat on our own bodies, screamed the soundless scream,
sweated blood –
in agonies which white men caused, damn them and their
      lives.

Yet you have still learned from them,
and turn your new craft to us. Rape. Bash. Kill.

We, your Sisters, newly learnt
that protection is possible,
that with you by our side we are safe,
that together, we are all safe,
must learn again . . .

Must learn to defend ourselves
from those who stand so close,
eat of our table, of food which *we* prepared,
must learn again to recognize the mad-dog disease
which is again the white man's legacy.
      ■

◄ One Day

Moving along Main St. /
   Whitesville /
Digging all them white faces /
   (Staring, or 'not staring')
Until I felt surrounded /
   Lost / bobbing on a sea I didn't know /
I began to concentrate so hard /
   (Head down)
On the lines and cracks
   Of the footpath

And I felt you / unknown Brother /
   Across the street /
Over the heads / cars
   Throwing me your glance /
Your salute / clenched fist /
   Smile . . .

Fellow Black /
   You were majestic /
Your sparks lit up the street /
   Whitesville /
And I was no longer moving along /
   But / Brother /
      Moving up!

■

◄ Rachel

Rachel died on Palm Island Reserve after a doctor refused
to treat her in the middle of the night. Departed: 15/2/74 –
aged 8 months

Named from the Bible /
That good and holy book /
Which came into this country
Along with Cpt. Cook
     And metal axes
     And beads and mirrors
     And money and guns.
Rachel never walked in the sunshine
Nor felt the wind breeze through her hair
Rachel never had a chance to see the things we see
Rachel didn't have a choice to be or not to be . . .

And the A.M.A. and D.A.I.A. will hide the worthless soul
Who, through 'benign neglect', deemed she would never grow
  old,
Though pledged to Hippocrates' Oath, he didn't give a care
  – May his evil deed haunt and follow everywhere –

For faster is forgiveness granted for he who strikes a blow
Than for a doctor who refuses help to a babe who doesn't
  know
That Racism is its enemy, and apathy the sword
Which sweeps away its tiny breath and delivers to the Lord.

Named from the Bible /
That good and holy book /
The people who brought it
Need to take a closer look . . .
     Suffer the little children . . .

■

◄ Final Count

The children are dying /
In terrible numbers of
Malnutrition and
Related diseases and /
We do not count their numbers
Amongst the brave dead of
Our revolution /
Yet their blood is surely spilled
As though shot upon the street /
Had they lived
Long enough to die.

We must count them /
We must count them /
For if we do not
They will have died in vain.

■

◄ Cycle

The revolution is conceived
as a babe in the womb;
It is, as a foetus,
An idea – a twinkle only
in men's eyes and a silent knowing
in women;
Yet it lives.

The revolution is alive
while it lives
within us;
Beating, making our hearts warm,
Our minds strong, for we know
that justice is inevitable –
like birth

Unaware of what they see,
They watch us;
We grow stronger and threaten
to burst our skin;
They do not realize
that the revolution
is near birth

That it threatens to spill
from this succoured womb
To the long-ready world
Which has not prepared
Even in this long time of waiting.

We do not always talk
of our pregnancy
for we are pregnant
with the thrust of freedom;
And our freedom looks to others
As a threat.

Yet we must be free, we know it,
And they know it,
For our freedom is not a gift
To be bestowed,
But torn from those
Who seek to keep us down.

We must stand up, raise our arms
To the sun, breathe deep the free air,
And our children
Cavort as new-born, trouble-free.·

The revolution lives. It lives
within us. Birth is imminent.
It cannot be bought off,
pushed back, held off.
The revolution will spring forward
As surely
As the child will leave the womb
— When it is ready;
We must make haste preparing
while biding our time.

∎

COLIN JOHNSON

◄   Colin Johnson, Bibbulmum, was born at Narrogin, WA in 1938. He was educated partly in an orphanage and later thrown on the streets of Melbourne when the promised employment was withdrawn. Colin pursued his writing to draw attention to the injustices, which finally made him seek a more humane aspect in Buddhism.

In 1959 he wrote a play called *The Delinks* and won a competition run by the University quarterly *Westerly*. With this encouragement to his writing he went on to to write a novel, *Wildcat Falling* (first published by Angus & Robertson, Sydney, 1965), which became runner-up for the 1966 Llewellyn Rhys Memorial Prize and was the first major success story for Aboriginal writings.

For many years Aboriginals lamented the departure from his land by Colin, who travelled to India and became a Buddhist monk for seven years. He travelled widely in south-east Asia, the U.S.A. and Britain. Upon his return he joined the Aboriginal Research Unit at Monash University in Melbourne, Victoria which was under the Directorship of Colin Bourke.

In 1979 he wrote *Long Live Sandawarra* (Quartet Books, Melbourne), and was joint author with Colin Bourke and Isobel White of *Before the Invasion: Aboriginal Life to 1788* (Oxford University Press, Melbourne, 1980). His latest novel is *Doctor Wooreddy's Prescription for Enduring the Ending of the World* (Hyland House Publications, Melbourne, 1983). *The Song Circle of Jacky and Selected Poems* has been published by Hyland House, 1986.

◄ Song Circle of Jacky

Jacky him been sit listening to the wind:
Jacky him been walk listening to the wind.

■

◄ They Give Jacky Rights

They give Jacky rights,
Like the tiger snake gives rights to its prey:
They give Jacky rights,
Like the rifle sights on its victim.
They give Jacky rights,
Like they give rights to the unborn baby,
Ripped from the womb by its uncaring mother.

They give Jacky the right to die,
The right to consent to mining on his land.
They give Jacky the right to watch
His sacred dreaming place become a hole –
His soul dies, his ancestors cry;
His soul dies, his ancestors cry:
They give Jacky his rights –
A hole in the ground!

Justice for all, Jacky kneels and prays;
Justice for all, they dig holes in his earth;
Justice for all, they give him his rights –
A flagon of cheap wine to dull his pain,
And his woman has to sell herself for that.
Justice for all, they give him his rights –
A hole in the ground to hide his mistrust and fear.
What can Jacky do, but struggle on and on:
The spirits of his Dreaming keep him strong!

∎

◀ Jacky Demonstrates For Land Rights

The last land rights' demonstration is over,
All the allies have gone home,
But black youth make their stand
On Capital Hill – feeding the magpies:
Finding there the Site of the Magpie Dreaming.

People come and people go,
Tourists ignoring the plight of our land,
But high flies the Black, Red and Gold,
High flies the Black, Red and Golden Sun.

People come and people go,
The youths stay on, broke and hopeful
Beneath the Black, Red and Golden Sun.
Sick of Redfern, sick of Fitzroy,
Sick of pigs, blows and booze,
Sick of sadness, filled with hope –
Going to stay on 'till they get their rights;
Going to stay on 'till we get our rights:
While people come and people go
Walking beneath the Black, Red and Gold.

The last land rights' demonstration is over,
All the allies have gone home,
But black youths make their stand on Capital Hill,
On the lost site of the Magpie Dreaming –
They are no longer there; the magpies have all gone,
All gone, have gone from the dreaming site
Along with Jacky and his kind.

■

◄ Jacky Hears The Century Cry

In 1914 I was young and creative:
Then I made my first attempt,
Tried bullets and bayonets,
And killed millions of myselves,
But not enough, I still lived.

I ached and pained,
Stayed in hospital for years,
But grew inventive:
I had to try again.

In the thirties, I used the aeroplane,
Followed it with careful plans of gas ovens,
Hacked and bombed and shot and cut,
In the last explosion thousands died to add
To the millions dead, but I still lived!

How to end myself, how to end this life?
I employed scientists and set them to work;
They discovered napalm and how it hurt;
Thousands died, but I still survived,
Planning the final solution to myself.
Jacky runs from such a terrible dread.

▪

◄ Jacky Sings Hit Songs

1

I know that I am –
No jargon, please –
I know that I am,
Water and earth
Mixed with a little wine.

Don't tell me who I am:
A child cries in me too often,
To have many illusions
My mouth curves,
In sadness these days.

I know that I am
Like a lonely child,
Locked in a black closet,
Long given up attempts to get out;
Huddled in the darkest, scary corner.

Don't tell me who I am –
A deserted hotel room,
A sink in one corner,
A wardrobe, bed and chair:
No poetry, only a Rolling Stone
Opened at Random Notes.

2

If you want me, try your jails,
In solitude, a bible for my love.

If you want me, walk along a street
Holding in each factory doorway,
Nothing, but your middle-class do-gooder fear;
Then stop, look down, right down –
An empty bottle, a sprawled black body,
Pink streaming urine stinking of your wine.

If you want me, follow the screaming siren
Rushing pigs to crush our anger –
Brother against brother 'till they come
And hustle away the debris of our hope.

If you want me, try your grassless parks,
In solitude, old men drinking life away.

■

◄ Reincarnation

You rise like the phoenix
From the ashes of your drunkenness,
Hands shaking, mind feeling the terror
Of the old year holding nothing but the next.
How often have we trodden these ways,
You and I, dark skins glistening
With the oil of our newest heroes, Crackerjacks,
Fast and furious on their feet.
How often have we walked these ways,
They flare in the sky summoning our people onward;
How often have we been this way,
The cricket team long ago going to British shores,
Finding them cold and dismal, bereft of gum trees.
We tread this way, mates, our paths
Splattered with women seeking something in our sadness,
To give their lives a sudden rise, perhaps a meaning.
Mates, we use our hands and feet,
And forget the toll in our lack of fullness.
How many have gone down beneath our fists,
Still we lack the sense of victory to complete ourselves,
Even though suits and ties now clothe the emptiness
Of our souls gone astray in the loneliness
Of maybe next year or the one thereafter.

∎

◄ Streets

In the swirling waters,
A brown face appears
And then is gone.
'A Koorie, a Koorie,'
I ask, my eyes
Seeking amid the whirlpools
A single unity
Which will make me
A wave swelling along
With a sudden
Quiescent ocean.

■

MAUREEN WATSON

◄   Born in the Beginning, Maureen comes from a large and well
known family whose care, concern and active participation in
the community has in no small measure meant much to the
contribution for change and new, positive direction in Aboriginal politics and freedoms.

Maureen travels extensively within Australia and overseas,
and is an accomplished actress and poet. She is widely known to
schoolchildren through her story-telling, poetry readings and
acting.

◄ Stepping Out

I'm stepping out, don't mess about.
Don't tell me to be patient.
I've been wedded, enslaved, white washed, and saved,
But now, I'm liberated.
I've been patted, and moulded, and shaped, and scolded
And I learned real fast how to please 'em,
I 'Yessir'ed, and 'No Ma'am'ed,
I was cursed and damned,
And all for no good reason.
I've been put up, and I've been put down,
By folks who were black, white, yellow or brown,
Treated like I wasn't human, just a puppet, a token,
But I healed my hurts, 'cause for better or worse,
Black woman's got spirit that's never going to be broken.
Been labelled all my life,
Black, woman, mother and wife.
And their labels formed the bars of my prison,
But I've got to set free, this person who's me.

'Cause now I've got a vision,
Their myths and lies are dead,
Not heaped on my head,
And their history is all outdated,
Different sex, different skin, can't change what's within,
'Cause now, I'm liberated,
And I'm stepping out, don't mess about,
Don't tell me to be patient,
No ifs or buts.
I don't walk, I strut,
'Cause now, I'm liberated.

■

◄ Female Of The Species

Whoever said I can't fly?
Why, Sisters, I can – can't I?
Whoever said, that because I'm a girl,
I'd be moulded and scolded by a sexist world.
Told me I could only be a mother,
Said I could never do things like my brother.
Well, here's mud in your eye,
'Cause Sisters, I can – can't I?
Why, Sisters, You told me, I could be free,
Showed me I could be, what I wanted to be,
Told me that I could liberate myself,
That I need never be left on the shelf.
Why, I can spread my wings and fly away,
From the depths, to the heights any night, any day.
Why, the whole wide world is within my reach,
I can learn or I can teach,
Why, I can dig ditches or write professorial theses,
'Cause me – why, I'm the female of the species.

And I've rewritten the story of the power and glory,
The wonder of being, the joy of seeing,
In every direction, my reflection,
In a million women's faces,
And I've found my place in a million different places,
For a human being, the female version.
And you know what?
It couldn't have happened to a nicer person,
'Cause I like what I see, when I look at me,
And I don't have to be, what I used to be,
I can be whatever I choose to be.
So you can throw out the book on your sexist theses,
'Cause me, why, I'm the female of the species.

■

◄ Memo To J.C.

When you were down here JC and walked this earth,
You were a pretty decent sort of bloke,
Although you never owned nothing, but the clothes on your
    back,
And you were always walking round, broke.
But you could talk to people, and you didn't have to judge,
You didn't mind helping the down and out
But these fellows preaching now in your Holy name,
Just what are they on about?
Didn't you tell these fellows to do other things,
Besides all that preaching and praying?
Well, listen, JC, there's things ought to be said,
And I might as well get on with the saying.
Didn't you tell them 'don't judge your fellow man'
And 'love ye one another'
And 'not put your faith in worldly goods'.
Well, you should see the goods that they got, brother!

They got great big buildings and works of art,
And millions of dollars in real estate,
They got no time to care about human beings,
They forgot what you told 'em, mate;
Things like, 'Whatever ye do to the least of my brothers,
This ye do also unto me'.
Yeah, well these people who are using your good name,
They're abusing it, JC,
But there's people still living the way you lived,
And still copping the hyprocrisy, racism and hate,
Getting crucified by the fat cats, too,
But they don't call us religious, mate.
Tho' we got the same basic values that you lived by,
Sharin' and carin' about each other,
And the bread and the wine that you passed around,
Well, we're still doing that, brother.
Yeah, we share our food and drink and shelter,
Our grief, our happiness, our hopes and plans,
But they don't call us 'Followers of Jesus',
They call us black fellas, man.
But if you're still offering your hand in forgiveness
To the one who's done wrong, and is sorry,
I reckon we'll meet up later on,
And I got no cause to worry.
Just don't seem right somehow that all the good you did,
That people preach, not practise, what you said,
I wonder, if it all died with you, that day on the cross,
And if it just never got raised from the dead.

■

◄ Black Child

Black child's soft mouth atremble,
Angry tears in innocent eyes,
Agony in a mother's heart,
As they hear the white man's lies.
Black child is hurt, and puzzled.
'But Mother loves you, Son', she cries.
But all a mother's love can't dry
The tears in a black child's eyes.
Child grows older, and he's off to school
Mother waves her babe goodbye,
Faltering smile upon her lips,
But tears shine in her eyes.
And there's anger in a brother's fists
And shame in a father's heart,
That he sees his people suffer so,
And a black child's world falls apart.
And he sees all the black man's truths,
Distorted by white man's lies
Poor innocent, helpless, wounded babes.
With tears in their big dark eyes.
Oh, I'd cut out my heart and lay at your feet.
And I'd rip the stars from the blue,
I'd spit on the sun and put out its light,
If I could keep all this hurt from you.
Flesh of my flesh,
And blood of my blood,
You never hear how my aching heart cries,
To a people too cruel,
Too blind to see,
The tears in a black child's eyes.

These breasts can fill and overflow,
They've suckled babies, watched them grow,
This womb, too, has given birth,
How dare you, then, to judge my worth.
By all the gods and powers that be,
That made woman and man,
You and yes, me,
Till they create another human race,
I spit, defiant, in your face,
Though you watch me die as you have done,
I will live again, in my daughters, my sons.
And you will hear my cry, even as you deny,
I, too, am human.
I'd spit on the sun and put out its light,
If I could keep all this hurt from you.
Flesh of flesh,
And blood of my blood,
You never hear how my aching heart cries,
To a people too cruel,
Too blind to see,
The tears in a black child's eyes.

■

JACK DAVIS

◄ Jack Davis, Noong-ah, was born in 1917, in Perth, W.A. With his first book of poetry *The First Born* (published by Angus and Robertson, Sydney, 1970) Jack firmly established himself as an Aboriginal poet shouting, sobbing, demanding that his song, the Aboriginal song against injustice, be heard. The opening cry was one of outrage and lament from which the title of his book emerged: 'Where are my first born, said the brown land, sighing.'

Jack Davis's family history is so typical, in so far as it is an experience shared by many Aboriginals: his mother was taken away from her tribe in Broome and reared by a white family; his father, William Davis, was also removed from his tribe and reared by whites. Such removal of children from the tribe was a common practice by white authorities in their 'assimilation' policy and as an aid in gaining psychological control over the Aboriginal population. No attention was paid to the desires of the Aboriginal family. Indeed, Aboriginals were denied any say in their affairs at all. The 'reserves' were concentration camps; the Aboriginals, the prisoners, the victims of their conquerers from overseas.

The Davis family moved to Yarloop, a milltown in the south west of Western Australia. There were ten children in the family and the mother displayed a special kind of courage, and self-sacrificing guts in the face of racial genocide.

Jack had eight years of education in public schools, then worked as a mill-hand, an engine driver, boundary rider and drover, which brought him into contact with the tribal people, and gave acute examples of the everyday ill-treatment and victimisation they suffered. While the squatter kings in their grass castles waxed fat, Jack witnessed their abuse of Black labourers who were forced to work without pay, apart from a few rations — dry bread or flour, camp meat, a stick of tobacco. If Blacks dared to kill cattle to eat, they risked death or at the very least, imprisonment, removal from tribe and family, and the ever-present fear of their children being taken away. These are some of the influences on the development of this poet's voice. He later furthered the cry for justice with *Jagardoo: Poems from the Aboriginal Australia* published by Methuen, Sydney, 1978.

In 1977, much to Aboriginal disgust, Jack was awarded the British Empire Medal for services to literature and the Aboriginal people. Aboriginals collectively believe no 'honour' can come from one as dishonourable as the thieving British Empire, believing instead that our, "Good on you, Bunji" or "Youai Moodjarng" is the greatest accolade we, the sovereign sons and daughters of this country, can bestow on one another. When this grand old 'grandfather' of the Aboriginal voice in print produced the plays *Kullark* (first performed in Perth, 1979) and *The Dreamers* (first presented by the Swan River Stage in 1982 and subsequently staged by the National Theatre Company of W.A., then taken on a six month national tour by the Australian Elizabethan Theatre Trust), Aboriginals recognised that here indeed was a voice ready to depict events as they were and, in many instances, as they remain and will remain until we all unite for justice and win by whatever means justice demands.

His latest play, *No Sugar*, received standing ovations when performed in Vancouver and Edinburgh in 1986.

◄ The First-born

Where are my first-born, said the brown land, sighing;
They came out of my womb long, long ago.
They were formed of my dust – why, why are they crying
And the light of their being barely aglow?

I strain my ears for the sound of their laughter.
Where are the laws and the legends I gave?
Tell me what happened, you whom I bore after.
Now only their spirits dwell in the caves.

You are silent, you cringe from replying.
A question is there, like a blow on the face.
The answer is there when I look at the dying,
At the death and neglect of my dark proud race.

■

◄ Aboriginal Reserve

The long low sweeping ground,
The horizon black in starlight
And somewhere now the sound
Of a child's cry in the night.

They stir a fire that is dying,
The sparks fly upward blending
With night and a people crying.
O where, O where is the ending?

The mind forgets tomorrow,
Eyes grow dull with the years,
Afraid of the heights of sorrow
And to fathom the depths of fears.

■

◄ Slum Dwelling

Big brown eyes, little dark Australian boy
Playing with a broken toy.
This environment his alone,
This is where a seed is sown.
Can this child at the age of three
Rise above this poverty?

The walls all cracked and faded, bare.
The glassless windows stare and stare
Like the half-dead eyes of a dying race. . .
A sad but strange, compelling place.

■

◄ My Brother, My Sister

There's a gleam of the moon on the man on the rim-rock:
His arm, lifted high, flashes down in an arc.
The kangaroo runs, spins, leaping and tumbling
And falls to the ground with a spear through the heart.

When they hunt in the swamp it's a piccannin morning,
Then the water-hen ripples away from her nest.
Oh, this harvest of food is truly God-given
For life has a purpose and love's at its best.

Then the sheep and the cattle came over the ranges:
They flattened the grasses and muddied the waters.
The uron* and carda crawled into the boulders
And the bigorda is hiding behind the full moon.

Come, brother, come into the townships and cities.
There's food and there's drink, all yours for the asking,
A house, near-condemned, some clothing to match it
And a Guv'ment man with his tongue in his cheek.

Come Marpoo, bring Jeeri: she's young and becoming.
She's frightened, we know, but we show her the way.
We show her the brute and the beast that is in us,
Then turn her loose in the city to play.

Oh, my people, my people! You are the changelings.
The neon lights flicker: 'Kia-ora Saloon'.
The kangaroo comes from the shop on the corner.
My brother, my sister, you are dying too soon.

*Uron – the bob-tailed goanna. Carda – the race-horse goanna.
Bigorda – the hill-kangaroo.

■

◄ Urban Aboriginal

She was born with sand in her mouth,
The whisper of wind in her hair;
They washed her clean in warm wood ash
And wrapped her in loving care.

She lay in the mould of her mother's arms,
She suckled her honeyed breasts;
She grew and she watched day turn to night
When you came out of the west.

You came loud-mouthed, with eyes cruel,
You made her a concubine;
Then flung her into a wilderness,
That beautiful Woman of Mine.

With murder, with rape, you marred their skin,
But you cannot whiten their mind;
They will remain my children for ever,
The black and the beautiful kind.

This poem was written in reply to a statement made by a Minister
for Aboriginal Affairs that urban Aborigines are not true Aborigines.
■

◄ Aboriginal Australia

to the others

You once smiled a friendly smile,
Said we were kin to one another,
Thus with guile for a short while
Became to me a brother.
Then you swamped my way of gladness,
Took my children from my side,
Snapped shut the lawbook, oh my sadness
At Yirrkala's plea denied.
So, I remember Lake George hills,
The thin stick bones of people.
Sudden death, and greed that kills,
That gave you church and steeple.
I cry again for Worrarra men,
Gone from kith and kind,
And I wondered when I would find a pen
To probe your freckled mind.
I mourned again for the Murray Tribe,
Gone too without a trace,
I thought of the soldiers' diatribe,
The smile on the Governor's face.
You murdered me with rope, with gun,
The massacre my enclave,
You buried me deep on McLarty's run
Flung into a common grave.
You propped me up with Christ, red tape,
Tobacco, grog and fears,
Then disease and lordly rape
Through the brutish years.
Now you primly say you're justified,
And sing of a nation's glory,
But I think of a people crucified –
The real Australian story.

■

HYLLUS MARIS

◄   I met Hyllus in Melbourne, where she lived and was then working on her book with Sonia Berg. The book, *Women of the Sun*, published by Penguin, became a resounding success after the award winning television series broadcast in 1982. It made dramatic potential of the Aboriginal historic mosaic.

   Hyllus Maris was a mature, able and determined protagonist for justice and Aboriginal rights. She employed her heart and poetry as well as her organisational ability to impart her feelings and her gifts. She died at an early age, a victim of cancer. A disease that has increased in frequency since the atomic tests of the 50s and 60s. Her love and her vision will always guide us.

◄ ## The Season's Finished

Outside the rain is falling down;
He hears it on the roof and the splashing
On the tin nailed across the window.
He feels the breath of the wind that blows
     between the cracks in the door
     and up from the floor.
The dog lies close to his feet
     shivering,
The wood on the fire is wet
     and hasn't caught yet,
     and the cold stings his toes.
He can hear his wife and kids in the next room
     coughing,
How he wished they'd stop.
He gets busy making tea and frying roti,
He opens the cupboard to get the plum jam
     but it's near empty. Damn!
How he wished the rain would stop;
No more picking peas,
No money, season's finished.

He sits and wonders what went wrong,
It's been this way since the day he was born.
All these things going round in his head,
Sometimes he wishes he was dead.
The wind moans, the air is colder,
The night comes down.
He blows out the candle and goes to bed.

■

◄ Spiritual song of the Aborigine

I am a child of the Dreamtime People
Part of this Land, like the gnarled gumtree
I am the river, softly singing
Chanting our songs on my way to the sea
My spirit is the dust-devils
Mirages, that dance on the plain
I'm the snow, the wind and the falling rain
I'm part of the rocks and the red desert earth
Red as the blood that flows in my veins
I am eagle, crow and snake that glides
Through the rain-forest that clings to the mountainside
I awakened here when the earth was new
There was emu, wombat, kangaroo
No other man of a different hue
I am this land
And this land is me
I am Australia.

■

DAISY UTEMORRAH

Daisy Utemorrah was born at Kunmunya in February 1922.
Her mother, of the Ngarinjin people of the Kimberleys, imparted
the knowledge of tradition and relationship with the complex
structure of the land in its totality.

Daisy, a literacy teacher and health worker, devotes much of
her life to writing the stories and working with her husband, also
a health worker.

Mary's plea

Where am I
You, my people
Where am I standing.
Take me back
  and hold my hand
I want to be with you.
I want to smell
    the smoke
        of burnt grass.

Where are you
    my people
I am lost;
I've lost everything; my culture
    that should be my own.

Where am I
The clouds
    o'er shadow me
        but my memories are there.
But I am lost,
    my people,
Take me back
And teach the things
I want to learn.

Is it really you my people,
The voices,
The soft voices that I hear.
■

VICKI DAVEY

Vicki Davey was born thirty-three years ago in Port Lincoln. She now lives in Adelaide.

Vicki has worked in various jobs as typist, telephonist, as a switchboard operator with government departments. In 1985 she became involved with Black Magic Radio, of which she says 'Black Magic Radio has seen the beginning of a national voice for Aboriginal and Islander peoples and has in turn given me a confidence to learn more about the electronic media'.

Her hobbies include music and reading, particularly history, and writing poetry.

The shadow of life

I meet you, but once
Like a stranger, I question your coming
You watch me, thoughtfully
Like a hungry lion stalking its prey.
Death follows, knowingly
Like a prostitute waiting for her man.
I saw Death take my friend into his arms
Like a satisfied lion, they disappeared into the darkness
Shedding tears, powerless
I watched your coffin sink into the earth
Cruel death, you never lose
Like a king, you choose the time
It is then, you come knocking, and your presence is felt.
Of mercy and love, you know not
Without feeling, you strike
I have felt your presence and know of your ways
Lurking, deep within the shadows of life, you create fear
But you let it be known, resistance is futile
Like the helpless cry of sheep awaiting slaughter.
We, too, must accept your coming.
■

ARCHIE WELLER

◄   Archie Weller was born on July 13th, 1957 in St. John of God Hospital in Subiaco, Western Australia. He grew up at Cranbrook, a small country town situated about twenty miles south of Perth in the bush country near the Stirling Ranges.

His mother, Helen Weller, of Scot ancestry, comes from a family that had a great joy in books and universal culture, which she passed on to Archie. His father, Claude Weller, comes from South Australia, and, as well as being a good mechanic, owned and worked a small farm, teaching Archie the value and respect for the land, the seasonal cycles and Aboriginal spiritual empathy with life and cultural aspects of creation.

Archie's grandmother came from the Port Augusta tribe; little is known of her background. He has two sisters, Jenny and Marcia, and a brother, Guy, all of whom are actively involved in the arts.

In his early teenage years, the family moved to East Perth, a poor area full of 'bikies, methos, migrants and Aboriginal families', where he began meeting up with Blacks, the *nyoongahs* in the area. He went through secondary education and later spent a year at the Western Australian Institute of Technology, where he dropped out after completing the first year and started to write his book, *The Day of the Dog*, published by Pan Books (Australia). His other books are *Going Home*, published in 1986 by George Allen and Unwin, and, most recently, he has co-edited with Colleen Francis-Glass *Us Fellas*, an anthology of Aboriginal writings.

◄ From the bottomless waterhole
calling Pidja! Pidja!
like the illusive wind, you came
and you settled in my hair.
As quiet as a thought
you crept upon my woman's leg
and we both dreamed a dream.
Like a pounding kangaroo
you kicked her to let us know
and then I could remember
that night, sleeping after the hunt.
Alone I was, before your pool.
How happy we were then;
how happy we are now,
spirit-daughter of mine.
■

◄ And now we watch you crawl, you crawl.
In the ashes of the dying fire
you leave your track.
It is time for your Grandfather to come
to name you from your mother's totem
for now, child, you are a woman.
■

◄ I am waetch.
Fast I run.
Fast like the wind.
My heart pounds out
a triumphant tune.
Laugh now, if you dare.
See me leap and spring,
for in my mind
I am home.
And in my dreams
I am free.
From the Grandstand massive crowds cheer,
and my mother's soft voice whispers
from the peace of the camp lagoon.

■

◄ The children play like Yukana
like happy bailer-shell people
from times of long ago.
In the waters of our country
like waves they crash upon the shore.
Here then gone. Boys then men.

■

◄ Willy-willy man
Winningarra.
My wild wind man
came to me one night
beside the quiet billabong
underneath a quandong tree.

■

◄ The rain comes over the hills,
like fluttering birds, it comes.
I stand in my brother's tears
happy as the running stream.

■

◄ Ho! Brother
Tread upon the wide plains.
Lonely rugged mountains
rule the land.

■

◄ Kinigar,
Murderer.
Where is mopoke?
Where is wildu?
Brave and wise men die.
The lifeless bodies
of children
and women
and warriors
strewn upon the ground.
For the star is red in the sky
but the ships are white on the sea
and cruel Kinigar has returned.

■

◄ Pinjarra warrior, where were you that day
when iron lightning and cruel thunder were born?
I cry for my woman.
I cry for my dead son
killed by the men as white as soft summer clouds.

■

◄ Spilt blood and tears like rivers flow.
Painful memories drift like sand
from the dry and empty creek-bed.
Our spirits go to the islands
disappear like the bullets' echoes
or the screams of dying children.
For, like the thunder, horsemen came
and bullets crashed like rain and lightning
into the midst of the dancing people
of the people gorged on cattle meat
that triumphant hunters had brought back home.

■

◄ Oh, Domjum!
My brother.
I weep for you.
As children when we used to play
and you were always the leader.
You beat upon
your skinny breast
and cried out in joy
as big as the sun –
as big as living.
But now
last night
they shot you as dead
as only dead can be.
Blood as red as the new day
spreading across your black back
and your brown hands white
with the dust of stolen flour.

■

◄ To the Moore River Settlement we now go;
  in the belly of the rumbling iron snake
  that has swallowed us up, legends laws and all.
  From the trees so tall and proud.
  The spirits of these trees call out,
  And from the coloured carpets
  scattered like lakes upon the grounds we love so.
  Dressed in rags we go, and with whiteman blankets
  as grey as my soul inside.

  ■

◄ New earth mother.
  From the ragged blankets –
  the ragged grey blankets
  and filthy sheets
  your child is born,
  from the whiteman's drunken lies,
  into the New Dreamtime.

  ■

◄ Once, when walking down the wet grey streets
  with the grey wet city all around
  I smell the bitter scent of gum-trees
  growing from the pious Bishop's ground.
  Behind stone walls, just as we of old,
  dying of religion and from cold;
  now they have made prisoners of you
  in this cold cruel concrete whiteman's zoo.
  Do you remember how under leaves like yours
  children from the tribe would gather to play
  and sing loud the songs of their father's fathers
  as brown hands made stories from the river's clay?

  ■

◄ These coloured lights
are not my stars –
and this is not my dance.
I sit in the shadows
listening to the whiteman's
jubilant corroboree.
In fine whiteman clothes I sit
and drink, or smoke the sweet drugs
that give whiteman shaky joy.
Yet I am the King of the coloured-light people.

■

◄ Yesterday old Nundah's eldest daughter's son
was smashed to screaming death upon the pavement.
His head shattered like the life
he had tried to understand
from his Grandfather's gentle murmurings.
Old legends, old laws, old ways, old folk.
Yet he – so young; his blood as red as ochre
splashed on the dancing Macedonians
with iron bars as hard as their youthful eyes.

■

◄ Wurarbuti

Wurarbuti, as aged as his land,
stare out to sea . . . the green sea you love
as much as your daughter, Nagranini.
A bird with many wings as white as gulls
sits upon the waters of your bay.
A wingless baby from her breast is born.
Wurarbuti, your warriors wonder
for from the baby strange ghosts appear.

Faces the colour of dead man's bones
and voices as soft as a woman.
And see? there's one
with hair like the sun.
We come here in peace, they seem to say.
Wurarbuti, you in all your wisdom
have never seen the magic of these men
with rocks that reflect like still lagoons
your images.
So laugh out loud.
That night around fires you eat the fish
all the sweating fishermen caught that day
and laugh and sing and dance – all brothers.
But the ghosts drink evil yellow water;
from men into children they become.
Smiling, the one with sun in his hair
gives Wurarbuti flat shining shells
the colour of fish and bright like the moon;
as round as the moon is at full.
Foolish Wurarbuti. Unknowing chief
from the rocks and tides and beaches *you* came.
You do not need Moorindunni's money.
My Nagranini! Nagranini!
Aaii! He has taken Nagranini
into the bushes: into her body.
The sun man – the magic man –
has killed my Nagranini.
Oh, sorrow, sorrow, sorrow.
Now angry Wurarbuti kill the sun.
To the beach the old chief swiftly runs
and kills a sailor dreaming of home,
who from the sea, like a fish had come.
But what is this?!
The white man's spears
make sounds like the cracking of hot stones
and now you fall to the blood-red sand.

Yet, swift as a stingray, your thrown spear
finds one more man.
they leave, the murderous brothers
leaving the old confused and the young abused.
But like the morning's tide they will return.

■

◄ Midgiegooroo

Midgiegooroo
with your hair as wild
as a wind-torn gum-tree's leafy head
and with your puzzled eyes as dark as night.
Beeliars chief
as brown as the earth
that your painfilled mother bore you on.
Today the men
with their pale white skins
and their fine gold-tasseled uniforms
will soon tie you to the iron-barred door
and with their spears
as fast as widgi
as unseen as the mighty eagle
until its wicked steel claws sink home:
they will shoot you
for defending your crying land.
And blood will flow
like the blood from the red-gum tree
would ooze from stone axe cuts
just as you
hunted
possums
when a boy
so long
ago.

■

CHARMAINE PAPERTALK-GREEN

◄ Charmaine Papertalk-Green. Born at Eradu, via Geraldton, Western Australia in 1963. Her mother came from the Wadjari, and her father from the Bardimaia tribes. She was educated at Mullewa District High School and matriculated from Bentley Senior High School in Perth. She is currently doing a B.A. degree at the Australian National University, Canberra.

Charmaine grew up in a family of ten children of six sisters and four brothers. They lived at Mullewa, a small white dominated wheat belt town in Western Australia. Never mixing with white children except in school sports and class where Charmaine says 'I wouldn't call it mixing', white children sat on one side of the classroom, Blacks on the other. Mullewa was a very racist town with separate bars. A little of 'Little Rock' U.S.A. style racism, and a lot of the 'apartheid' oppression that white Australia's 'Eminent Persons' so roundly and loudly condemn in Africa.

Charmaine's father was a shearer, now a sandalwood contractor. In the early years, her mum worked at the Mullewa hospital as a domestic from the age of fourteen. The family faced the usual depressing environment out of which the children developed a sense of their own pride of place, a love and respect for cultural things. Their parents taught them to use their personality to overcome their oppression and to use their education to expose Australia's shameful and shabby heritage.

Charmaine's interests include writing poems about her people, and meeting Aboriginals and whites interested in the Aboriginal situation. Her poetry was included in *Australian Women Poets*, edited by Susan Hampton and Kate Llewellyn, Penguin Books, Melbourne, 1986.

◄ Are We The Same

Have you starved?
seen your mother flogged?
or your father hopelessly drunk?

Your world is not mine
Your belly has always been full
violence was seen on the Telly
not down the street
Your mother was hit behind doors
where she was too ashamed
to scream for help
What would the neighbours think!
They hid all this from you

I come from another world
One you will never know
You may try to understand
But never will.

■

◄ Wanna Be White

My man took off yesterday
with a waagin*
He left me and the kids
to be something in this world
said he sick of being
black, poor and laughed at
Said he wanted to be white
have better clothes, a flash car
and eat fancy
He said me and the kids
would give him a bad name
because we are black too
So he left with a waagin.*

*Waagin: East Coast word for 'white woman',
derived from 'white gin'.

■

◄ Pension Day

They sit under the gumtrees
waiting for the Post Office to open
looking cleaner than any other day
Some yarn and laugh
while others sit silently
They don't say what
they are gonna do
with their money
There's no need
They all end up at
the club
laughing, drinking and fighting

It's Pension Day
▪

◂ No One To Guide Us

Feeling down
depressed
wondering why
What is happening
in this society?
Police bashings in Roebourne
John Pat dies
There is no Justice
Suicide in Broome
another in Meeka
All young Aboriginals
Dying for what?
Feeling down
I don't understand
what is happening
Where are the spirits
Of our Ancestors?
Of our people?
To guide us.
■

LAURY WELLS

◀   Laury Wells was born in 1938, in Walgett, New South Wales. Laury had a primary school education of a sort typical to most Blacks in the south west of New South Wales in the late 40s and early 50s. A short biographical note would hardly suffice to give a glimpse of Laury's life. For that, we have to wait for him to write his life story which he has begun. In his own words, he says:

'My father was an Englishman. My mother came from a long line of Aboriginals but, to give you a better understanding, I'd better start at the beginning . . . Great-Great Grandfather Green came from Ireland and married a tribal Aboriginal girl. They had several sons and daughters, Jim, Tom, Annie and my Grandmother, Anne Green, all brought up and taught proper Aboriginal values, which my English Grandfather had learnt and kept great respect for. Granny married a Norwegian. They had several children, one of whom is my mother, who was also taught proper respect for Aboriginal ways. As I said in the beginning, Mum married an Englishman so my name is Wells. Real mix-up, isn't it!!!

'After Dad died (I was fourteen) I left school to help support the family. I carried the swag with Don Nolan for years, doing all kinds of bush and station work. During this time, I self-educated myself to a small degree and finished up driving big rigs, plant operating and doing mechanics. Working and living with Aboriginals, I learnt to make spears and boomerangs and how to hunt and live off the land. I made bark canoes, carved emu eggs, and have been writing short stories and poems since I was fourteen. I am still single, live on my own in a fully furnished house and am waiting for the right girl to come along . . .'

◄ Distress Upon The Farm

'Don't try and make that home made brew'
She pleaded on her knees,
'You'll end up getting injured dear'
She cried hysterically.

'We have some money put away
It's profit from the farm,
Please buy a jug instead my dear
Before you come to harm!'

But no he would not listen
And went and made the brew,
Then filling up a gallon jar
He spilt some on his shoes.

His wife heard frantic sobbing
And rushed down to his aid,
She found his shoes both eaten off
Caused by the brew he made.

His feet were raw and blistered
With all his toe nails gone,
And in a daze he asked her
'Oh what the hell went wrong?'

His feet are coming on just fine
And now he's moving round,
He went as she first advised
And bought a jug in town.

∎

The Nomads

The night draws in with the setting sun
And shadows very long,
A slight breeze stirs through the grass and burrs
Like the note of a mournful song.

And the dingos howl in the mulga scrub
In search of a water hole,
And wurleys gleam from shining beams
Off a rising moon of gold.

A dead snake sways from a broken limb
As figures move around,
By the fire's and moonbeams' rays
The nomads settle down.

■

Prelude

The track is my companion
A quiet eternal friend
For so alike together
We have no journey's end.

I find joy in roving
This land eternally
Beyond each lofty mountain
And valley I must see.

The track is my companion
Whichever way it lies
And I'll remain a Pilgrim
Until the day I die.

■

◄ The 'Sorcerer'

He broods of pleasant days gone by
As he squats in the hot, white sand,
Feeling a weariness through his bones
In this vanishing Never-land.

The cares of the tribe on his shoulders
Like the weight of a mighty stone,
And he sadly sighs 'neath the burning sky
As he eases his aching bones.

He'd like to sit as the others do
With his young wives by his side,
And have some younger one carry the woes
Of his swiftly vanishing tribe.

He knows his race is nearly run
And his old heart's filled with dread,
If there's no successor within the tribe
Before the old man's dead . . .

But teaching another may never occur . . .
With the young men going away,
His magic is strong, but he cannot prevent
The despondent going astray.

Rejecting their age-old-mysteries
Spanning thousands of years,
Knowledge as old as the land itself
Brings the 'Sorcerer' close to tears . . .

They'll not survive when their skills have failed
And the women are barren and worn,
The piccaninnies will be too few
With scant-new babies born.

Once sacred laws are vanishing fast
And when their totems are gone,
There'll but remain the elder's wail
And the spirit's dying song!

The symbol and cause of the change, is plain
As the tribes go one by one,
And the 'Sorcerer' knows in his wise old head
That his own tribe's nearly done.

Intruders stealing their land of birth
By force and oily tongue,
Bloodguilt ones who deserve the law
Of the pointed bone, and 'sung'.

Compelled to live on petty reserves
A blow to their dignity,
With initiations less each year
And their sacred corroborees.

Way out in countless far flung spots
The tribal ways have fled,
In place of wild-bush tucker, now
It comes in tins instead.

And scattered through the once pure bush
Are bottles, tins and cans,
Given by the irresponsible
To the natives of this land.

Diseases quite unknown before
The cruel invaders came,
Continue their terrible carnage
Of heartbreak, death and pain.

Serving the whites and apeing his ways
And forced to follow his law,
Hurts the elders of the tribes
And will wound a great deal more.

Huge money hungry companies
Raping endlessly,
The sacred sites, the bush and earth
Of the Aborigine.

The poisoned flour and guns are gone . . .
But things are much the same,
The trespassers are hunters, still
The black man's still the game.

The fight's been a long and bloody one
But the tribes have tried all ways,
To live as they did, in a now spoiled land
As they did in their carefree days.

His race is run, the 'Sorcerer' knows
And soon he'll be laid to rest,
And his sad heart yearns – there was a youth
Who'd pass the 'Sorcerer's test. . .

He broods of pleasant days long fled
As he squats in the warm, white sand,
Feeling a weariness through his bones
In his cherished native land.

■

REX MARSHALL

◄   Rex Marshall was born on 16.7.1943 at Grafton, New South Wales. His tribe is Thungutti/Gumbaingeri. Rex spent his first sixteen years at Baryulgil Reserve absorbing the differences between the Black reality and 'over-town' situations. He attended St. Joseph's Primary School, South Grafton, and Baryulgil Primary School until he reached sixth grade.

After leaving school, he determined to commit his life's work toward gaining a reasonable level of existence for Blacks. Baryulgil was a hotbed of politics since the Hardy company had an asbestos mine smack in the centre of the Reserve. The asbestos tailings, dust from the mines, were used to spread over the roads. Of course, many of the Aboriginal mine workers, as well as members of their families, suffered asbestos dust poisoning and many died. Rex joined with fellow Aboriginal activists, notably Gary Williams, Kevin Wyman, Tony Koorey, Michael Anderson, Gary Foley, Billy Craigie, Paul Coe and many other young men and women who set up the Aboriginal Embassy in 1972. The Aboriginal Embassy highlighted, internationally, the racist oppression and covert genocide of Aboriginals. Rex has since worked continuously in Aboriginal affairs. In 1973, he was elected as a representative on the first National Aboriginal Consultative Committee and held this position for four years. In 1979/80, he was Director of Aboriginal Cultural Education for the Kempsey Youth and Cultural Centre. He is presently the Administrator for the Coffs Harbour Aboriginal Family Centre. Between poems, he attends various functions in his capacity as a Justice of the Peace. He is also the Vice-President of the Murri-winna Gardens Aboriginal Academy, a member of the Durri Medical Service, Kempsey, and a member of the North Coast Institute of Aboriginal Studies.

◄ Burrel Bullai

'Burrel Bullai!' Our old people believed
That you had the power of calling them back,
To here, where the wattles and the gums are fresh
And green, and the country air is very clean.
At the bottom of your mountain,
Where the Nulla Creek flows
Lived the Thungutti Tribe of years ago;
They always knew that you were very near
Whenever they went hunting,
With their boondies and spears.
'Burrel Bullai!' Standing tall
Our people will always hear you call,
No matter wherever they may be;
In the city, and the country, or by the sea;
You tell of love and sharing and giving –
That is a big part of Goree living.
'Burrel Bullai!' No matter where we may roam,
We will always call Bellbrook our home.

■

◄ Buddgelin Bey

Dark clouds are gathering a way up in the sky
The storm is coming very quickly
And Ma keeps a track of it with a watchful eye
Holding her axe in her hands, two feet firmly on the ground
At last she gets ready to make her stand
Against the wild wind and rain blowing around
According to her custom she must cut the storm clouds
While waving the axe and chanting out loud
A lore that was handed down to her tribe
This custom she has carried out with such pride
With a final shout of Buddgelin Bey
The wild storm is blown away.

■

◄ # Little Brown Jacks
Nyimbung

Late in the evening when the children are at play
Those little brown Jacks start making their way
To where the boys and girls are having fun
Before the going down of the sun.
They grab the children's hands, and join in the games
And have a good time; Just the same
The brown Jacks our children cannot see,
For they are only visible to adults like me;
They don't mean harm to anyone,
And only come to have some fun.
So while your child is at play,
Please watch them in every way,
For little brown Jack is ever so near;
He is a person they do not fear.
Because nyimbung are little children at heart
They really give us Elders a start;
These little men are older than Time
And do not belong to a nursery rhyme,
Nyimbung are a part of our Aboriginal Lore,
And are little people we really adore.

■

PAM ERRINARON-WILLIAMS

◀   Pam Errinaron-Williams was born at Longreach, Queensland. Pam's mother is from the Goreng Goreng tribe. Her father is of Irish/Maori descent. Married, with one child (a daughter), Pam is widely acclaimed as a singer and traditional dancer. She grew up in Queensland and comes from a large family who are all musically talented. At the age of five, she began training as a competitive swimmer, travelling extensively with her father to swim in competitions. She was Queensland Champion for her age grouping. In 1971, she went to a catholic boarding school and engaged in competitive trampoline sports and became Queensland Women's Champion for some years. In 1971, Pam joined in a Land Rights group which was begun by a catholic priest called Mick Hayes. Father Hayes believed that the apartheid, and its inherent denial of human rights, in Queensland could only be altered by changing the system that took control of Aboriginal lands and placed Aboriginals in exile, refugees in their own land. This group ultimately became the Aboriginal and Islander Catholic Council.

Pam is currently studying for an Arts Degree in Canberra and is part of a musical trio, developing her Aboriginal dancing.

(N.B. Aboriginals in Queensland *still* live in refugee camp areas where oppressive racial laws ensure that our people remain exiles in our own land.)

◄ Torn Apart

(for all Black women taken from their mothers)

Is this what you've done to us
took us away
from the warmth
of mother's arms
screaming with pain
I cried for years
seeing my mother
cling to the last feel
of my arms
as I clung to her

at that place
they taught me to
rise when the bell rang
strip the bed and mop the floor
so long away
I thought of you
and how I missed you all

all I wanted
was the feeling of love
that only the family
have for you
they told me you were unfit
to care for me
but I know
you would have loved me
and that's more
important than anything

I've searched for you
through piles of papers
and long corridors
of unseeing faces
with racist blocking walls
I cry for you at night
my mother
so strong and silent
I wail for the loss
and the pain
they inflicted on us both

now I sit lonely
here in this darkened room
remembering how you were
gentle dark face
lined with sorrow
did you sit as I
sometimes do
and think of how
much I might have missed you

I have a daughter now
olive skin like yours
and eyes so black
you fall into their pools
I look at her
and remember you
and how I might
have looked to you
but it's ok
and though I never
knew you mother
I remember your arms
warm and gentle
rocking me to sleep
at night
when darkness
sometimes left me frightened.

■

FRANK DOOLAN

◄   Frank Doolan is of the Kamilaroi tribe. The Kamilaroi were a
powerful force in opposing the early invasion of their land,
holding off the settlers, 'black police', the constabulary and army
as the colonialists struck the tribes with terrorist tactics to
destabilise the region. The tactics used, such as burning women
and children alive, cutting their throats and genitals and
watching the victims run and flap about before collapsing, then
throwing them still alive into triangular fires, is attested to by
white historians and humanitarians of the day who protested to
the Colonial Office. Such representation was, of course, ignored
since 'peaceable settlement' was the stated policy of the Colonial
Secretary and British Government. It was to be achieved as
expediently as possible even by the annihilation, if necessary, of
the Kamilaroi. The Kamilaroi are still resisting the invasion of
their lands as this book goes to press.

Frank Doolan, a 'grass-roots' Black, is a gentle, sensitive spirit,
with the kind of strength displayed by the Kamilaroi people that
will challenge tyranny whatever the odds against him may be.

Born in Bourke, New South Wales (a racist town of ill-repute,
that people of goodwill and conscience avoid where possible),
Frank, one of five children, went to third form, gained his School
Certificate in Sydney. In this he was helped by his stay at Kirinari
Hostel which is a special educational hostel built for the purpose
of helping Aboriginals gain access to an educational level denied
them by the prevailing attitudes in the school system.

Frank Doolan intends to find a publisher for his book of poems,
and hopes to do a B.A. at Sydney University.

◄ Who Owns Darling Street?

Whiteman dressed in your fancy clothes
I'm laughing at you as you look down your nose
And sign your petitions to keep out the Blacks
Call us lazy bludgers who live off your tax
You say we're the cause of this Black and White strife
But white backstabber you don't hurt me with your knife
For though we're the Blacks you love to ill-treat
Let me ask you Whiteman, who owns Darling Street?

Whiteman you came such a short while ago
Erecting your fences where once wildlife roamed
Draining natural resources with your cattle and sheep
Abusing the land by playing for keeps
Your thirst for land and your love for money
Makes me laugh at you Whiteman as I think it's funny
Really it is, don't we have more right
To sign a petition to keep out the whites?

So think it over Whiteman you're wrong again
And all your petitions don't mean a thing
For though we're the Blacks you love to ill-treat
Let me ask you Whiteman, who owns Darling Street?

■

◄ The Last Fullblood

The old man's almost gone
When he goes the culture dies
Cause he can't read or write
And I reckon it's a crime
Our stories are passed on
By word of mouth or paintings
But vandals wrecked our caves
And the old man's got trachoma

Yeah and I can't tell my kids
Cause I don't know much myself
The old man can't remember
He ain't in the best of health
Don't you reckon it's a crime
In the name of all that's good?
Cause the old man's almost gone
And he's the last fullblood

The old man used to tell me
When I was just a kid
Of happier days, how things have changed
Now he's the last fullblood
But the old man isn't bitter
Would you blame him if he was
You broke his spirit long ago
Now he just lives for grog

The old man doesn't want
A big head stone on his grave
Just bury me with my spears 'n' things
Is all he's asked of me
I might hit the wine myself
Pretend it doesn't hurt
Cause the only land he'll ever own
Is six cold feet of dirt.

■

The Whiteman Is The Judge

You've locked so many Blacks away
But you'll never hide the truth
White law enforcement in Australia stinks
You're left without excuse
We represent just two per cent
Of the total population
With the highest rate of imprisonment
Due to your discrimination

Your law just doesn't cater
For the dispossessed Blackman
Cause I could get six months inside
Just for spitting in Queensland
In New South Wales the premier State
The premier doesn't care
Visit Bathurst, Goulburn, Long Bay gaols
See how many Blacks are there

Yeah how many Blacks have you bashed to death
All in the name of the law?
The whiteman is the judge
But it isn't a crime to be poor
So look down your nose at my secondhand clothes
But where the hell's the justice
Hold seminars, put Blacks behind bars
With your racist laws enforcement

Proud boys in blue don't we all know
Why the whole world calls you Pigs
And how the whiteman's the oppressor
Cause the whiteman is the judge

■

Oodgeroo Noonuccal (Kath Walker)

◀   With her first book of poems, *We Are Going*, Oodgeroo became the first Aboriginal poet to have a book published and became one of the best selling poets. Of greater significance to Blacks, her works brought national and international focus to bear on the oppression of Aboriginals and raised the question of human rights and equality. Hers was virtually a voice in the wilderness and was, without a doubt, a major contributing factor in the recognition of citizenship rights for Aboriginals following the 'Yes' vote in the 1967 Referendum.

Oodgeroo, of the Noonuccal, spent her early childhood years on Stradbroke Island. Born in 1920, some eight years before the last recorded massacre of Aboriginal people at Coniston, N.T., she left school and became a 'domestic', being paid two shillings and sixpence a week. When the second world war broke out, she served as a telephonist in the Australian Women's Auxiliary Service and later trained as a stenographer.

Her intensive efforts to gain social and political change have never wavered. She held the position of Queensland Secretary of the Federal Council of the Aboriginal Advancement League and served on the executive of a number of other organisations. For many years she has fought for an 'Aboriginal Charter of Rights' which seeks to alter the conditions under which Aboriginals live. Such changes include a reduction of the Aboriginal infant mortality rate, an end to slave-like work conditions and to the dreaded 'pass laws' which force fathers and mothers to be separated from their children, and a cessation of the virtual exile in the guise of 'service' to remote stations or cattle empires. Her cry was a challenge to the society that victimised the Aboriginal and stole Aboriginal land and resources.

'Give us welcome, not aversion
Give us choice, not cold coercion
Status, not discrimination,
Human rights, not segregation . . .'

Oodgeroo later wrote *The Dawn is at Hand*, published in 1966 by Jacaranda Press in which she said in 'Assimilation – No! . . .'

'Change and compel, slash us into shape,
But not our roots deep in the soil of old.
We are different hearts and minds
In a different body. Do not ask of us
To be deserters, to disown our mother,
To change the unchangeable.
The gum cannot be trained into an oak.

In 1970, her third book of poems, *My People*, was published by Jacaranda Press and was testimony to the strength of this proud woman and her unquenchable fire for gaining justice and rights for Blacks.

She wrote *Stradbroke Dreamtime*, published by Angus and Robertson in 1972, and *Father Sky and Mother Earth*, published by Jacaranda Press, 1981. On the 11.11.1986, I met her at a writers' conference, where she was speaking on a panel of 'Writers Against Nuclear Armament'. She spoke of a new age, a new terror as well as of the old terrors that continue for Blacks in this country. Her poems, if one listens carefully, speak about universal love, universal rights, universal dignity, and love and peace for this land. Like her, we wonder if white Australia will ever hear and heed what this poet says.

Oodgeroo, now 66 years old, says 'Old' is an honourable word in our world. In the white world it's a disgrace. And, to prove her point, she made her acting debut in the role of 'Eva' – a powerful, spiritually moving old woman and one of the camp Elders – in the 'Fringedwellers', a film based on the novel by Nene Gare.

Despite the fact that she has flown to many countries, many times, she admits to a little apprehension for she was once involved in a 'hijack', of which she says, 'I was *more* than a little nervous, but they (the hijackers) treated me with the utmost respect when they realised that I was an Aboriginal'.

◄ Colour Bar

When vile men jeer because my skin is brown,
This I live down.

But when a taunted child comes home in tears,
Fierce anger sears.

The colour bar! It shows the meaner mind
Of moron kind.

Men are but medieval yet, as long
As lives this wrong.

Could he but see, the colour-baiting clod
Is blaming God

Who made us all, and all His children He
Loves equally.

As long as brothers banned from brotherhood
You still exclude,

The Christianity you hold so high
Is but a lie.

Justice a cant of hypocrites, content
With precedent.

■

Gooboora, the Silent Pool

For Grannie Sunflower Last of the Noonuccals

Gooboora, Gooboora, the Water of Fear
That awed the Noonuccals once numerous here,
The Bunyip is gone from your bone-strewn bed,
And the clans departed to drift with the dead.

Once in the far time before the whites came
How light were their hearts in the dance and the game!
Gooboora, Gooboora, to think that today
A whole happy tribe are all vanished away!

What mystery lurks by the Water of Fear,
And what is the secret still lingering here?
For birds hasten by as in days of old,
No wild thing will drink of your waters cold.

Gooboora, Gooboora, still here you remain,
But where are my people I look for in vain?
They are gone from the hill, they are gone from the shore,
And the place of the Silent Pool knows them no more.

But I think they still gather when daylight is done
And stand round the pool at the setting of sun,
A shadowy band that is now without care,
Fearing no longer the Thing in its lair.

Old Death has passed by you but took the dark throng;
Now lost is the Noonuccal language and song.
Gooboora, Gooboora, it makes the heart sore
That you should be here but my people no more!

■

◄ The Unhappy Race

The Myall Speaks

White fellow, you are the unhappy race.
You alone have left nature and made civilized laws.
You have enslaved yourselves as you enslaved the horse and
      other wild things.
Why, white man?
Your police lock up your tribe in houses with bars,
We see poor women scrubbing floors of richer women.
Why, white man, why?
You laugh at 'poor blackfellow', you say we must be like you.
You say we must leave the old freedom and leisure,
We must be civilized and work for you.
Why, white fellow?
Leave us alone, we don't want your collars and ties,
We don't need your routines and compulsions.
We want the old freedom and joy that all things have but you,
Poor white man of the unhappy race.

▪

The Past

Let no one say the past is dead.
The past is all about us and within.
Haunted by tribal memories, I know
This little now, this accidental present
Is not the all of me, whose long making
Is so much of the past.

Tonight here in suburbia as I sit
In easy chair before electric heater,
Warmed by the red glow, I fall into dream:
I am away
At the camp fire in the bush, among
My own people, sitting on the ground,
No walls about me,
The stars over me,
The tall surrounding trees that stir in the wind
Making their own music,
Soft cries of the night coming to us, there
Where we are one with all old Nature's lives
Known and unknown,
In scenes where we belong but have now forsaken.
Deep chair and electric radiator
Are but since yesterday,
But a thousand thousand camp fires in the forest
Are in my blood.
Let none tell me the past is wholly gone.
Now is so small a part of time, so small a part
Of all the race years that have moulded me.

■

◄ Municipal Gum

Gumtree in the city street,
Hard bitumen around your feet,
Rather you should be
In the cool world of leafy forest halls
And wild bird calls.
Here you seem to me
Like that poor cart-horse
Castrated, broken, a thing wronged,
Strapped and buckled, its hell prolonged,
Whose hung head and listless mien express
Its hopelessness.
Municipal gum, it is dolorous
To see you thus
Set in your black grass of bitumen –
O fellow citizen,
What have they done to us?

■

◀ Time is Running Out

The miner rapes
The heart of earth
With his violent spade.
Stealing, bottling her black blood
For the sake of greedy trade.
On his metal throne of destruction,
He labours away with a will,
Piling the mountainous minerals high
With giant tool and iron drill.

In his greedy lust for power,
He destroys old nature's will.
For the sake of the filthy dollar,
He dirties the nest he builds.
Well he knows that violence
Of his destructive kind
Will be violently written
Upon the sands of time.

But time is running out
And time is close at hand,
For the Dreamtime folk are massing
To defend their timeless land.
Come gentle black man
Show your strength;
Time to take a stand.
Make the violent miner feel
Your violent
Love of land.

■

JIM EVERETT

◄ Jim Everett, Mawbana Pleregannana, was born on Flinders Island, Tasmania, 1942. Jim went to school in Victoria and left at Grade 7 and started his working life as a telegram boy. Later he worked as a factory hand and fisherman, joined the Regular Army, tried life out as a merchant seaman, rigger, truck driver, Aboriginal community worker, public servant and has been a very capable Aboriginal political activist.

He was the first ever Tasmanian Member to the Aboriginal Arts Board, was the Co-ordinator for the Council of Aboriginal Organisations in Tasmania, National Secretary of N.A.I.W.O.L.D.A. (National Aboriginal and Islander Writers Oral Literature and Dramatists Association), State Liaison Officer for Aboriginal Affairs in the Tasmanian Government, and was acting Chairman of the Aboriginal Arts Board.

Mawbana writes poetry, short journal articles, children's short stories and plays. One of his plays, written jointly with Richard Davey, *Put Your Boots On*, was performed by the Tasmanian Aboriginal Theatre Group at the 'Salamanca Arts Festival' in Hobart, Tasmania.

◄ Old Co's

He had been there all his life, at the Corner
And could remember back as far as the big wreck
The Cambridgeshire, all hands lost at Thunder 'n' Lightnin'
He could remember the Old Co's talkin' about them,
The dead, and what to do, where to lay 'em.
Layed 'em in the old school house finally.
But there was the wreck, the salvage of cargo
They reckon there was rum in barrels, and pianos
Pianos washed up on the shores for any who want 'em,
Still, it was the rum what was the main one.
He told me that the Old Co's buried the rum,
in the sand down one end of Thunder 'n' Lightnin' beach.

Never could find it again he said, damned sand shiftin'
Not many years later he said he started work, huntin'
Flamin' possums, had to eat 'em too after awhile
Most Old Co'es did anyway, he said
Better eatin' than rock wallaby or scrub tucker
And a sight better 'n eatin' salt meat all 'a' time
'Course, he said, that later on when he joined the boat
An island trader, tucker was near fresh all 'a' time
With greens and milk and bread
And in port a feller had strong drink,
Not to mention another face besides seein' Old Co'es all 'a'
    time
Everyone travelled by boat them days he said
From island to island and over to Tassie
A lot of Corner Co'es had their own boat
Used 'em for visitin' 'n' Birdin', and gettin' tucker
From whoever had a mind to trade
Some even visited the school on Badger Island
Run by Lucy and Elizabeth, couple Old Co'es livin' there
Fine women those Co'es, made land claim for us they did,
Land Claims for the Corner Co'es they said, it's a right
He remembered all that about the Old Co'es he said
Ain't seen anything get better for the Corner Co'es
Worse he said, damn well sent all sorts of right 'ns over
Measurin' heads 'n' askin' silly questions
We told 'em all sorts've stories, straight faced like
And the Corner ended up with a community officer
Or some damn thing anyway his record stands
'Cause when they started forcin' Corner Co'es to leave
Go from our island 'n' live in the city
That's when the Corner Co'es got the nerves proper he said
He'd been through it, all the Corner Co'es know
Give an inch 'n' lose a mile, got no land left now
Hardly got a name other than that'n put on us
Seen it comin' he said like all the Corner Co'es
Old Co'es, with tears and hurtin' all over, us Old Co'es
Just knew that our Young Co'es would have to fight

Pick it up and put our name on it
And our face 'n' our feelin' for the land
'Cause when they're Old Co'es too they'll look
And remember, he said, just remember about Old Co'es
And this we give 'm, their rights and the big job
To keep our people goin', as leaders: as Old Co'es.

■

◄ Ode To Salted Mutton Birds

Mutton birds! I like 'em I'll eat 'em any way.
Skin 'em 'n braise 'em and serve 'em on a tray.
Stuff 'em 'n bake 'em, and serve 'em with sauce.
Or put 'em over the coals, on a spit of course.
I like 'em grilled, I like 'em fried.
And there's plenty other ways I've tried.
But salted birds, just scar and boil.
With carrots, spuds and swedes as well.
It's the best way known to man or beast.
To eat mutton birds and have a feast.

■

◄ Rest Our Spiritual Dead

Red, black and yellow are the
colours of our band,
Black is for the people
of this Southern land.
Yellow is for the mighty
sun life giver in the sky,
And red is for our people's
blood so onward we survive.

Rest our Spiritual Dead at this sacred place,
We are returning you to rest here in peace,
Your people here today know you feel our love,
Rest our Spiritual Dead here at Oyster Cove.

It's a long, long time we've struggled for your peace,
Those who hindered your return filled us with unease.
But your spirits gave us strength to bring about this right,
We now return your spirits to this sacred site.

Forever after this day we will protect this land,
This very place you return to is now our sacred ground.
Now this place called Oyster Cove is where your spirits rest,
Tell the world that Oyster Cove is Aboriginal blessed.

Red, black and yellow are the colours of our band,
Black is for the people of this Southern land.
Yellow is for the mighty sun life giver in the sky,
And red is for our people's blood so onward we survive.

■

◄ The White Man Problem

It's 1982 and 200 years gone by,
Aborigines have fought yet continue to lose.
The white man came and spread his plague,
With them came their rights we did not choose.
We cannot control this thing engulfing us,
Yet onward we must stand our ground of life.
And remain true to our beliefs as they evolve,
In hope, the white man problem becomes less rife.

We can teach our ways but few whites want,
For they believe their technology is best for man.
And on they succeed in changing our ways of life.
With 'civilization' widening the span.
They cannot see how they are wrong in this,
For blinded minds of glory and power.
Tis the power which prevents their gain in life,
And creates the white man problem turning us sour.

The white man problem is greed and rape,
And their ten commandments they ever break.
Why have such laws if they prevent their aims,
Forever strived by whites alike.
The answer must be that whites with power,
Exploit the poor and down of their kin.
That dog eat dog is white history known,
That the white man problem is not just his skin.

■

IRIS CLAYTON

Iris Clayton of the Wiradjuri tribe was born at Leeton in the Riverina district of New South Wales. Iris grew up on the banks of the Murrumbidgee River, the south-west border of Wiradjuri country, in 1945.

Her Grandmother had a lot to do with her upbringing, helping to develop Iris' interest in creative art and oral history. There were nine children in the Clayton family. The 'Aboriginal Board' – Welfare – took the eldest six children away from the mother as was the common practice then to 'de-stabilise' and 'assimilate' Black children and families. It was during this era that many Aboriginal children became the 'stolen generation'. 'Welfare' authorities deliberately kept parents apart from their children, had our children adopted or put them in 'wardship' which in real terms meant slavery, being paid a shilling and sometimes two shillings and sixpence a week 'wages' while working as cooks, housemaids, gardeners, stockmen, and quite often being sexually abused and used as concubines.

Iris and her sisters went to Cootamundra Aboriginal Girls' Home where the 'training' began. Her two brothers were sent on to Kinchela boys' home. As Iris says: 'We weren't allowed to see our parents. We were really cut right off. They tried to wipe us out in one hit, our whole family background. We were brought up with white outlooks. Never taught Black history or anything and if we used Wiradjuri (Aboriginal) words at the home we were dreadfully punished. It's a sad story really. A lot of the girls died from schlerosis of the liver, through alcoholism, after they left the home. Some turned to prostitution, lots of them committed suicide. They just couldn't cope with the brutal system and being Black, knowing Black, and not being allowed to be Black. A lot of those who were put into "service" were sexually abused, and when they fell pregnant, were sent to Parramatta Girls' Home as "uncontrollable".'

Iris has six children and, after studying Aboriginal History, began work with the Australian Institute of Aboriginal Studies in Canberra. Her main interests are painting (oils), poetry, writing and letting the world know about the injustice, racism, slavery and abuse that still happens in this country today.

◀ Kidnappers

There were nine little blackfellas
having fun and running free
along came the welfare
said this just cannot be
he grabbed the little blackfellas
sent them all to the homes
to train them all as servants
to slave in gubbars' homes
and when the little blackfellas
grew up to be eighteen
some of them were shy and timid
and some of them plain mean
now some of them have children
of their very own
and they don't want
to see them sent
to the bloody training homes
They all hate the whiteman
with his racist laws
and they all keep the whiteman out
when he knocks up on their doors.

■

◀ River Bidgee

No one knows how long he's been there
Twisted, old ravaged beyond repair
Father to many, too many to count.
His dying will be a terrible account
Perhaps if the damage is quickly mended
His shores and banks strongly defended
Old River Bidgee need never be
Another lost legend of the Warrajarree.

■

◄ The Black Rat

He lived in a tin hut with a hard dirt floor,
He had bags sewn together that was his door.
He was a Rat of Tobruk until forty-five,
He was one of the few that came back alive.

Battered and scared he fought for this land,
And on his return they all shook his hand.
The price of fighting for the freedom of man,
Did not make any difference to this Blackman.

He returned to the outback, no mates did he find,
If he had a beer he was jailed and then fined.
He sold all his medals he once proudly wore:
They were of no use to him any more.

Confused and alone he wandered around,
Looking for work though none could be found.
The Anzac marches he badly neglected,
Would show to his comrades how he was rejected.

He fought for this land so he could be free,
Yet he could not vote after his desert melée.
And those years in that desert they really took their toll,
He went there quite young and came home so old.

This once tall man came from a proud Black tribe,
Died all alone – noone at his side.
■

◄ The Last Link

The walls were the colour
of dark burnt brown
matching the skin of
the old blackman
the cracks in the wall
he did not see
but this old man
loved to talk to me

He told of the days
when he was young
when once the tribe
of his deeds they sung
how they hunted and roamed
free as the winds
he told of his battles
losses and wins

I looked at the walls
all covered in grime
and thought to myself
this is a crime
this old blackman
is our living history
so full of legends
the dreaming and mystery

As I was thinking
the old man talked on
moaning his sorrow
of days lost and gone
he asked if I knew
how we came to be
I answered my nanny
told that legend to me.

He said to me my days
are near done
let's move outside
to sit in the sun
I'll have to tell you
about tribal law
but noone uses
them anymore

I was the best hunter
did I tell you before
I shook my head
I wanted to hear more
he looked at me
so sad and forlorn
I could tell that his heart
was broken and torn

With tears in his eyes
he spoke of his wives
then sadly he told how
both lost their lives
he cried for his children
a girl and two sons
and how they were killed
by whitemen's guns

This old blackman
with his stories untold
said let's move inside
I'm now getting cold
he asked me to call
again in the morn
but when I got there
his soul it had gone.
■

DEBBY BARBEN

◄   Debby Barben was born in Carlton, Victoria on 16.10.1959.
She has an older sister who was born in 1957. At the age of six,
Debby was 'fostered' to a non-Aboriginal family in the Manly
area where she remained for a few years until that 'placement'
broke down irretrievably and she was returned to the Bidura
receiving home. At thirteen years of age, she was placed with a
foster-family on the South Coast. That placement lasted for three
months and Debby was returned to Bidura, then to Lynewood
Girls Home before being transferred to Newcastle Girls Home.
Finally, Debby went to a family on the North Shore, where
apparently, given a chance to further her development, she is
working in Residential Care and youth work. She studied Welfare
at Milperra College and has been employed as a welfare worker
for sixteen months. Her aspirations are to find her father, and I'm
sure someone in our community will pick up the clues she has
provided, write her biography, and one day have a country house
for kids with nowhere to go.

Do you know or think you do
You sit there talking and preaching
Patting yourself on the back
    Have you been through it.

◄ To Look Yet Not Find

To look yet not find
I feel a heavy weight
My mum i see
With everlasting hope, someday;
    hope to meet

Many names has she
I wonder if she knows who
    she is
To open the door i must find
    the key

Hope! i won't give up
One day there's going to be a clue
And each other we shall see.
■

◄ Four White Walls

Four white walls
Three bed boards
Two showers
Three loos
One person
    Me

Up down, up down
    I pace
My screaming and banging
    the only sound
Help i think, i'll go insane

Up down, up down
    got to get out
let me out, but they don't
    hear my shout

Oh please let me out
My four hours is done
and yet they have won.
■

◄ Eight Beds, Eight Lockers

Eight beds, eight lockers
Eight cupboards, eight people
Three young, five old
Yet noone to trust

Green, Yellow, Red and Brown
Silver, Grey and Black
Books, magazines and papers
Yet noone or nothing to
    relate to.

Eat, drink and talk
Vacuum, wash and wipe
Yet no real communication,
No trust, just nothing
    but objects.
■

◄ Do You Know What You're Saying

Do you know what you're saying
Have you heard it yourself
How much do you practise
    What you said

Do you know or think you do
You sit there talking and preaching
Patting yourself on the back
    Have you been through it

If you sat and listened to one
    that had
and to someone that was
    themselves
that's when you will
    learn something.

■

DYAN NEWSON

◀ Dyan Newson was born Dyan Elizabeth Shaw in Launceston, Tasmania in 1952. Dyan spent her early years of childhood and schooling on Flinders Island. After leaving school, she worked as a shop assistant, factory worker, sawmill hand, secretary, and Child Care Co-ordinator with Aboriginals. She has been actively involved with Aboriginal issues since 1976, and is currently serving on the Aboriginal Education Community Committee, Secretary to the Tasmanian Aboriginal Centre, Launceston Branch, and Member of the Tasmanian Aboriginal Child Care Association.

She is married with six children whose ages range from six years to seventeen years, and still finds time to write and share her poetry through various small journals.

◄ Crowther – Ours

They're only bones the whiteman say,
So why then all the fuss,
'Cause they're our people,
And they're ours,
Because they are of us.

They want to cremate them whiteman way,
We WANT to have our say,
I wonder what would happen,
If we interred whiteman, Blackman's way.

I can now feel the spirits,
They are peaceful, yet so sad,
They're pleased they'll soon be resting,
OH! what a shocking time they've had.

And when the day is over,
When it's been done Blackman's way,
They'll be thanking us in Dreamtime,
For being glad we had our say.

■

◄ Turnabouts

There is a group of blacks about,
Who are not black at heart,
I call this group the Turnabouts,
The blacks that have gone white.

They use our kind to get revenge,
It's wrong and we all know,
They are two-faced, these TURNABOUTS,
They won't give us a go!

They're really nice when face to face,
And always in a crowd,
But cannot wait till we are gone,
So they can speak out 'loud.

It's hard enough for blacks right now,
We do not need that kind,
Why! most of us are strong at heart,
While they are weak of mind.

It takes all kinds to make a world,
And this we all do know,
They cause all kinds of problems,
And we have enough right now.

There is no need to worry,
For they'll get their just deserve,
There is no room for TURNABOUTS,
MY GOD THEY HAVE A NERVE!

If you're born black,
That's what you are,
You cannot change a thing,
We should all be proud of what we are,
AND KEEP THE BLACK WITHIN.

■

STEPHEN CLAYTON _____

Stephen Clayton is Wiradjuri and was born at Leeton, New South Wales in 1956. Stephen is the younger brother of Iris Clayton. He served in the Australian Army, and now works for the Health Commission at Liverpool, N.S.W. He is very involved in Aboriginal youth and community work.

He is married, and has three daughters, maintaining their interest in Koorie history, culture and the Wiradjuri language. Like Iris Clayton, he has always been interested in oral history and poetry, and hopes one day to see his writings and poetry published as a book.

The Good Old Days

Back in 55, when I was just a lad
My father was a farmer
Working someone's land.
Although I never knew him
I know that this is fact,
It's written on my birth certificate
Occupation – Farmhand.
They call this time 'The good old days'
I wonder if he'd known
He'd been working in the noon day sun
On land
His ancestors once owned.

■

◄ Soul Music

Dancing to vibrations of unheard melodies
Swaying to the sound of silence in his ears
The deaf man danced alone.
People hearing, laughed
'Poor bastard', they cried. 'He doesn't even know,
The music stopped, long long ago!'
The deaf man kept on dancing
Laughing to himself
'If only they would listen, if only they could know,
How it feels to hear the music
Real music.
The music of your soul!'

▪

◄ Boom Time

Calculated figures, estimated lives
Science and computers make calculated lies
Men are only digits on little blue screen games
When the button is pushed, no one remains.

▪

◄ Redfern At Night

7 pm in Redfern, apprehension showing
Faces of the whiteman, pensive, paranoia growing
Fear fills his mind, prejudice his heart
Thinks – those black bastards – bastards of the dark
Avoiding all the back streets, running to his house
Streets empty quickly, silence, only blacks venture out.

11 pm in Redfern, pubs begin to close
Police with clubs swinging, blacks bloody nose
Arresting blacks at random, no reason given
Said, not permitted on the streets, not after eleven.

11.30 pm in Redfern, tension growing
Faces of the blackman – bleeding, confusion showing
Anger fills his mind, hatred in his heart
The bastards keep on hitting, because his skin is dark
Taking all the back streets, sneaking to his house
Streets empty once more, uneasy silence,
Not even blacks venture out.

■

◄ Sunshine Prisoner '470'

I

Through bars he looks, longing for freedom;
Sad and dejected he ponders his crime,
Regretful and sorry, impatient with time.
Fitter, more active. All look as one,
Clothed all the same, in a State Institution.
David's his name, but no one will know,
For in prison he's called, simply, – '470'.
Two children at home, but no longer a wife;
She's left him this time, for more of a life.
Grey walls, barred windows, birds flying by,
Guard towers, high fences: all in his eye.
People talking together, but feeling alone;
Someone crying for family, for friends, to go home.
Traffic outside, horns blaring away –
Maybe the children will visit today?
Dark walls, cold bars, no warmth found in here.
Wonders how he will last,
There is still one more year!

II

Two years in prison believing in Rights
(So cold in this cell, especially the nights)
Protests, and protests: what is the use?
This is *our* land. Must *we* suffer abuse,
Truncheons and clubs, dogs and police,
Fighting and kicking? We only want peace!
Laws in this State cannot guarantee
If your skin is black there'll be equality
Night time once more; time to dream
Of what it is now, and what it has been.
Dreams of a day when we'll be as one
Standing proud and aloof, people of the sun.
Dreams of a land, and rights to roam free
As our ancestors once did 'tween desert and tree;
Not chained by laws that deny us ourself,
Not seeking riches, nor material wealth.

III

Visiting day, and the children are here,
But there are no smiles on faces so dear.
'Daddy, Daddy', his little girl cries,
'We're going away'. And tears fill his eyes.
'Down South we're going. We're going today.
Please, Daddy, Please don't let them take us away'.
Desperate now, heart breaking in two,
The children leave crying, 'Daddy, we love you'.
Just one more fence, and freedom sublime
Be with the children, won't leave them this time.
A shot rings out breaking the night.
A religious man talks, of what's wrong and what's right.
Two children are crying. David has gone –
His body to the land, his soul to the sun.
A little girl turns to his mother to say,
'Mummy, is this Daddy's Land Rights, is it too much to pay?'

▪

ROBERT WALKER

◄ Robert Walker was born at Port Augusta on December 25th, 1958. He died aged twenty-five years, between the hours of 4.30 and 5 a.m. on Tuesday, August 28th, 1984, in the confines of the prison at Fremantle.

Robert Walker was the fourteenth child of a total of fifteen children born to Linda Walker (née Giles) and Anzac Walker. Linda and Anzac lived on Point Pearce Aboriginal Mission in Yorke Peninsula, leaving Point Pearce shortly before Robert's birth to go to Andamooka, the opal fields. Port Augusta had the nearest hospital facilities and it was there that Robert was born on Christmas Day, 1958.

Being born on Christmas Day, being part of a big Aboriginal family, having a hard-working, caring Dad who taught the children that speaking up for their rights was not arrogance, that human dignity and pride in family and self was a good fine thing, to survive, to defend one's rights was full of portent for Robert and his family. When Anzac died, Robert moved between the families, sometimes staying with Mum, his big sister Charlotte, or with his Uncle Moonie and Aunt Edna. Robert used to cry to be with his other uncle, Andrew, an Elder of the Kokatha, so Robert absorbed the tribal influences and mores of the old people in the camps as well.

Later, his mother, Linda, took the family to Adelaide, where Robert underwent the usual schooling for Blacks; white kids beating up on him, spitting on his lunch, denigrating him, and he starting hitting back. Later he was getting into 'trouble', having run-ins with police, and he had a taste of Yalata prison and then, inevitably, Fremantle gaol.

In Western Australia, Aborigines make up 3% of the population, yet at any given time their numbers in prison are never less than 30% of the prison population. Such an alarming proportion of Aborigines in gaol does not mean that Aboriginals are more criminal than whites or immigrants, but rather reflects the attitudes of a racist society, a government policy of discrimination and, of course, the attitude of a police force that has targetted a minority group with the approval and support of the government of the time. It all goes back to the initial denial of Aboriginal rights and justice that began with the Letters Patent which approved the setting up of Western Australia and South Australia, providing that 'Aborigines retain usufructuary rights to hunt, that land areas be set aside for Aborigines, that 15% of all land sales within the colonies be set aside for Aborigines' benefit, and 1% of the gross national product be set aside for the benefit and education of Aborigines.' Of course, as soon as the areas mentioned attained status, they immediately ignored, or repealed the Letters Patent obligations and, instead of honouring the Imperial Directives, they dispossessed us of our lands and, driven, shot, poisoned like dogs and kangaroos, the few remaining of our people were placed in 'reserves', concentration camps, refugees, exiles in our own country.

Robert Walker, the poet, has been given this longer biographical space for he, the poet, was seeking answers to universal questions about the denial of humanity and callous indifference to Aboriginals' lives in this country; a fear, a hatred even, of Black skins and Black culture. What are the causes? Why does such inhumanity persist? Is it a leftover of superstitious fear in the minds of European Australians, a sort of race memory fear carried over from the times they tortured women and burnt them, fearing 'curses' and 'witches'? Why such callous indifference to the lot of Blacks in this country, when the whites respond to the 'boat people', the starving peoples in Africa? How can a young poet understand why the Australian Government refuses to give medical funds to Blacks dying from Hepatitis B by the hundreds, saying there are no funds available, while announcing billion dollar grants to defence or the Bicentenary? There can only be one answer, an intolerable bitter racism in the ranks of the Australian Government and white society.

Isolated, subject to fear and hatred made even more intolerable by the claustrophobic walls of the prison cell, Robert Walker cut his wrists and began playing his guitar. He didn't intend to die, his wrist slashes weren't that critical. His personality unerringly dictated that he protest his treatment, that he force someone to take notice.

Someone did. At about 4 a.m. on Tuesday, August 28th, 1984, prison officers removed him from his cell. Emerging from the cell to the landing, he noticed the officers and began screaming in mortal fear. In a grassed area within the prison confines and within full view of a large number of prisoner-occupied cells, Robert Walker was held by officers and beaten with fists, boots and truncheons. In evidence later given, witnesses said . . . 'the screams were the kind to make hair on the back of your neck stand up. Every time Robert screamed the officer would hit him with the truncheon . . . the impression I got was that the . . . officer . . . was damn terrified that Robert would wake the whole of Fremantle up' and . . . 'there must have been over eighty blows'. 'Walker was not resisting at any time', 'His whole intent seemed to be to stop being hit'.

After seventeen or so such minutes on the lawn area where the beating took place, an injection of Largactil was thrust into Robert's body. His body went limp. He was handcuffed and taken away. At 5.15 a.m., Dr. David Bockman pronounced that life was extinct. A post mortem conducted on the day of death did not find the cause of death and described minor injuries.

Meanwhile, after hearing over the radio the news of her son's death, Linda Walker sought to have an independent autopsy, and sought the return of her son's body for burial. The State Prisons Department refused her request and tried to arrange cremation of the body. Finally, a second autopsy was conducted in Adelaide which found that Robert Walker died from 'acute brain death due to an obstruction of the blood supply to the brain caused by compression of the neck'.

Subsequent autopsy testimony given to coroner McCann was in agreement that the injuries to the body were consistent with force 'of a restraining nature', and, under cross-examination, conceded that he couldn't exclude that all the injuries to the body, including the fatal injury, were caused by numerous baton blows, kicks and punches as described by witnesses. Coroner McCann dismissed the evidence of prisoner witnesses in their claim of a 'brutal and unlawful assault'. In his finding the coroner, assessing the evidence of the 41 prisoner witnesses, said that, 'it is clear that in most cases they spoke of what they believed to have occurred . . . clear observation must have been difficult. The very prolonged struggle together with the screams and yells of the deceased must have had a profoundly disturbing effect on the inmates.' Ultimately it was found that 'the death arose by way of Misadventure', i.e. 'death caused by another unintentionally and in the course of doing something lawful'.

Finally, sometime, somehow, somewhere, white Australia has to come to terms with, and accept the fact that Black Australia was not settled peaceably, nor was it *terra nullius*, wasteland and unoccupied, as declared by Captain James Cook in 1770. In twentieth century maturity Australians should seek to rise above the psychology, the moral malaise of the convict heritage which has been so effective in allowing white Australia to maintain the lie of *terra nullius*, and to continue to parasitise Aboriginal land, Aboriginal resources, Aboriginal heritage without redress to justice and human dignity.

Robert Walker is not the only case of death in a prison, but his case represents a cry for justice and humanity. His call was upheld by Pope John Paul, who in his address at Alice Springs in November 1986 stated 'acknowledgement of the Land Rights of a people who have never surrendered those rights is not discrimination'.

Robert's sister, Charlotte Szekely, wrote to me and said, 'Robert's spirit isn't really here – not in the grave here in Adelaide. It's over *there*. In Fremantle Prison in the pool of blood. Aboriginal culture, the spirit can't rest until evil is stopped.' Grandfather Koorie replied to questions, saying, 'The spirit is a cycle. Robert Walker, Dixon Green, Tony King, Charlie Michaels, Eddie Murray, John Pat and the many tens of thousands of our people who have died in custody, or around waterholes, in the bush, return to their people to help the people survive, to face the enemies of humanity who have forced two hundred years of war, poverty and terror upon us. Robert Walker, his love, his *Nghulli*, is back with the Kokatha people.' He then wrote his poem to Robert Walker, 'Never blood so red'.

◄ Life Is Life

The rose among thorns
may not feel the sun's kiss each mornin'
and though it is forced to steal the sunshine
stored in the branches by those who cast shadows,
it is a rose and it lives.

■

◄ Solitary Confinement

Have you ever been ordered to strip
Before half a dozen barking eyes,
Forcing you against a wall –
ordering you to part your legs and bend over?

Have you ever had a door slammed
Locking you out of the world,
Propelling you into timeless space –
To the emptiness of silence?

Have you ever laid on a wooden bed –
In regulation pyjamas,
And tried to get a bucket to talk –
In all seriousness?

Have you ever begged for blankets
From an eye staring through a hole in the door,
Rubbing at the cold air digging into your flesh –
Biting down on your bottom lip, while mouthing
                    'Please, Sir'?

Have you ever heard screams in the middle of
               the night,
Or the sobbings of a stir-crazy prisoner,
Echo over and over again in the darkness –
Threatening to draw you into its madness?

Have you ever rolled up into a human ball
And prayed for sleep to come?
Have you ever laid awake for hours
Waiting for morning to mark yet another day of
               being alone?

If you've every experienced even one of these,
Then bow your head and thank God.
For it's a strange thing indeed –
This rehabilitation system!

■

◄ Unreceived Messages

Am I dreaming?
There you are.
Here am I.
. . . But your gaze
  Is beyond me.

> You are speaking,
> Your words are clear.
> I am speaking
> You do not hear.
> Inside – I move disturbed.

'I know you'
You echo: 'I know you'.
I reach out – but touch not.
My body still – still my body,
And still again I have failed
To communicate.

> My feet are walking,
> My mind recalling the words we spoke
> To one another – but not at all.
> Sorrow seeps through my shell
> Touching me – and I turn with joy.

In the line for lunch
I drift into oblivion again,
Weary from my efforts
To reach you – to know you
Like you say you know me.

The key turns – the day dies.
And once again I am born.
A child gasping for his first breath of life,
Crawling weakly from a plastic egg
To surface in a prison cell.

The pen – automatic
Like the beat of my heart.
Pain – a stranger to me –
Stops all but my heart.
Acid tears burning chips of egg shell.

I feel
And write life in every stroke.
The threat of death in every still moment.
Time circles above me like a vulture,
Then crawls on like a dying man.

Sleep – the semen of death
Draws me into its lust.
The night dies – and once again I am conceived
Oblivious to the life outside of my shell
For again but a foetus – awaiting release.

■

Okay, Let's Be Honest

Okay, let's be honest:
I ain't no saint,
but then again,
I wasn't born in heaven.
Okay, Okay!
So let's be honest:
I've been in and out,
since the age of eleven.

And I've been mean,
                hateful
                and downright dangerous.
I've lain in my own blood
in hotels
boys' homes,
and cop shops.
I've cursed my skin:
not black, not white.
Just another non-identity,
fighting to be Mr. Tops.

Yeah, so I'm called a bastard,
an animal, a trouble maker;
whilse my accusers watch my brothers smashed,
thrown into dog-boxes drunk, crying for the dreamtime
My memory is still wet with my mother's tears,
flowing by my father's grave.
Just another black family
alone and lost in the race for a dime.

As early as I can remember,
I was made aware of my differences,
and slowly my pains educated me:
either fight or lose.
'One sided', I hear you say.
Then come erase the scars from my brain,
and show me the other side of your face:
the one with the smile painted on with the colours
      of our sacred land you abuse.

'One Sided?' Yeah mate!
Cop it sweet 'n all.
'After all, you stepped out of line
and got caught.
So take it easy,' you say,
'You're not like the rest.
You have got brains and a bright future,
there's no battle to be fought.'

But that don't tell me what I want to know.
So tell me: why do we have to stand in line?
Why do we have to live your way, in subtle slavery
to earn the things that once were free?
Why do I have to close my eyes,
and make believe I cannot see
just what you are doing:
to my people – *OUR PEOPLE* – and me?

Well, bloody hell, Mate!
It ain't one sided at all!
Come read the loneliness and confusion
on the walls of this cell of seven by eleven.
Yeah, okay, I'll be honest:
I ain't no saint.
But then again,
I SURE WASN'T BORN IN HEAVEN!

■

GRANDFATHER KOORI

◄   Born in the Beginning in the heart of the red, sandy Mallee country in Wiradjuriland, somewhere near Ivanhoe. Tribe, Wiradjuri-Nghulli: *Murar ar ao Radthuri*. Red Kangaroo.

At school he excelled in nature studies, graduating with a Master's in life, a professorial branch in the sciences and innumerable credits in visionology.

These days he is satisfied to live his life, or rather, resigned to living his life in a haze of grieving despair as he searches in his impossible quest to find a potion, a solution or a psychic phenomenon of such magnitude as to be able to pierce the armour of ignorance, bigotry and impotence suffered by those afflicted with the atavistic malady of racism.

At our last meeting, he was kicking up dust on the Bornung and pointing, 'singing' a storm for the English 'Tall Ships' and Joh.

◄ Never Blood So Red

Never blood
so red so red
never blood so red
as blood of the poet
the Kokatha poet
who lay in the pool
so dead.
Never blood
so red so red
in Fremantle gaol so red
it glistens on batons
walls and feet
red drops on the warden's head
never blood
so red so red
never blood so red
as blood of the poet
the Kokatha poet
whose cries for justice
bled
whose cries for justice
bled.

▪

◄ Massacre Sandhill

The rain the rain the rain
the rain upon the hill
the three horsemen came
the three horses
the rain came down in clouds
and cried
the rain the rain cried
until it washed the blood
back into the land again
the rain the rain cried
until there was only the drought.

■

The Song In The Symbol

Look Look!
Look at the back
the dollar piece
there in the whiteman's hand
tinkling in corroboree
its own song sweet
our land
our country
Nghulli!
Murar a o-Murri
our *meat.*
The big red 'roo
looking to the mob
our mob
saying what to do
'keep hopping up
you mob
keep coming follow me'
he says 'keep hopping
you mob hopping
for scales to justice weigh
keep hopping follow me
you mob
we haven't lost the fight
one day we'll make the Rules
again again
and set our country right
again again
we'll set the Rules
stop murder of the trees
giving people *proper* rights
in *proud* land nuclear free
we'll keep our country hopping right
we'll keep the whole lot true
keep hopping up you mob
keep coming keep hopping up keep coming
there's work for you to do!!!'

■

GRAHAM BRADY, LUKE ROMA, STEVE BARNEY

◄   Grateful acknowledgement to Cheryl Buchanan, the publisher of *Murrie Coo-ee*, a collection of writings and poetry of our people in Queensland, for permission to publish these poems. Luke Roma, Steve Barney and Graham Brady are from families widely known and respected for their community activities and Land Rights support as well as their direct opposition to the draconian 'Queensland Act' which still operates and which denies equal opportunity and human rights to the majority of Queensland Blacks today.

GRAHAM BRADY

◄ Voice From The Bush – Through Me

Beautiful, O so beautiful
This feeling comes up from the
   ground,
and from everything around me
Ho'Nulli-gooda yundoo gudday'
(Great spirit come to us)
The ground is alive,
It speaks to me and you night and day
The trees are alive,
Don't hurt them only use them when
   necessary
Please brothers and sisters
don't kill for fun! or hate!
Only when necessary.

Always have respect for the land and
   sea
The feeling has always been here,
It only takes you to realise it
We are higher than all that's here
A Nulli-gooda said so.

(No. 1 hunter) Mulla-minya, don't kill
   too much you can't eat
Take what you need and no more.
(My babies) Nargoo gungle Natasia,
Narjic, Dennis and all my young blood
Grow up strong and listen.
Don't be afraid – our old people are
   with us.
If anything should happen to us, it is
through our own carelessness
or it was meant to be.
You have only one mind
Use it in your own right and possible
   way

We can only give you advice or show
   you
If we think you are wrong
Everything that belongs here was put
   here so that
We can live –
And we lived.

The bush can be hard
If you do not know how to use it –
Or use it wrong
We are all one people
With one great spirit – please
   remember
Ho Nulli-gooda yundoo guddayga
   gurrijgoo dooena
(Ho Great Spirit be with us and never
   never leave us).

  ■

LUKE ROMA

◄ I picture your face
and have visions
Of a beauty.

That is uncomparable
to anything
Except, a sun kissed rose
in the early morning mist.

■

◄ I drink your love
as I would
a cool mountain stream.

For I was lonely
Now I pray
that the spring
Does not run dry.

■

STEVE BARNEY

◄ Vision

My mother came to me
 in a vision,
  My mother was crying
  because, she told me,
  She was tired of
  being hurt,
She was tired of carrying
  the heavy loads,
  The steel buildings,
  the cement paths,
  and road made of
  bitumen running all
  over her body,
She asks me to help her
  to stop them taking the blood
  from her veins,
She beckoned me to heed
  her call,
For my mother is slowly dying
  and I will not stand back and
  watch them kill her,
Help me now my brother
  to care for our mother,
Because before I lose my
  cultural identity,
  I will lay in my mother's arms.

■

◄ Black People Cry

Black People Cry
and the white people wonder why
Some really try to understand
This strange human, the aboriginal man

Some wonder what is it this man wants
Is it to relive the past, with tribal hunts
What is it, this thing, they call the dreamtime
Come, don't be afraid of what you might find
Look! white leaders, do you see a broken race
Then look again, what do you see in their face
Look closely now, at the sparkle in their eye
Justice, equality and land, no longer, will the black people cry.

■

JOY WILLIAMS

◄   Joy Williams was born in Sydney in 1942 and named Eileen.
Joy is one of the 'stolen generation' children. Aboriginal children
removed from their mothers were placed in homes and made
over to be 'assimilated'. To this end they were trained to be
'house servants, maids, cheap labour and stock boys'. She was
removed in 1942 from her mother Doretta Williams upon the
signed authority of the Aborigines Welfare Board. In her
immediate family, children from four successive generations
have been removed from their parents. The official document
that records Joy's admission to the home reads '. . . to take the
child from the association of Aborigines as she is a fair-skinned
child'. Little or no attention was paid to the right of the mother to
her child or for that matter the rights of the child to the mother.
The committees of the Aboriginal Protection Board and Welfare
Board were made up of conservative white men who made the
rules affecting Blacks, rules that were callously indifferent to
Black humanity and Black life. (The white *community* was more
covert.) Joy was originally sent to Bomaderry Children's Home,
and at the age of six to a 'white' institution.

She 'came out' at sixteen, after having gone through the school
system about which she says, 'I came bottom in the State for
sewing. I came second in the State in English . . . but of course
that was never mentioned.'

Joy gave birth to her first born daughter, Julie-Anne Joy on
October 2nd, 1964. Julie-Anne Joy was taken from Joy at ten
months. Joy is still looking for her daughter and so far has traced
her to Singleton, New South Wales. Joy also now has another
daughter and a son.

Joy has worked for the Aboriginal Medical Service and is
currently a B.A. student at Wollongong University, NSW, and is
President of the Committee Against Racial Exploitation
(C.A.R.E.) on campus as well as the Convenor of the Committee
to Defend Black Rights in Wollongong. She is active in Link-Up,
an organisation based in Canberra, but operating throughout the
states, that searches out official records, 'linking up' children

and parents who were forcibly separated by the Aboriginal Protection Board and State authorities.

With the help of Link-Up, Joy finally traced her own family living at Erambie Mission, Cowra, in 1984, after 42 years of enforced separation.

◄ Rachel

I think of all the treasures of the earth
                                      I think of you,
I think of long, cool Summer nights
                                          I think of you,
I think of Beethoven's Pastoral –
                                        and I think of you,
I'll remember you, little girl,
I'll remember your tears,
I'll remember your love when I thought no one else loved me,
I'll remember you playing with a puppy –
                                     I'll remember you loved me.
Loving you was the easiest emotion I felt,
Hating you because you were a child came as easy.
■

◄ A thousand years ago I loved you,
I held out my hands and
Used a million words to woo you,
Slowly you came closer and, for a brief moment, held me.

Then came a storm between us,
I looked for you and found you nowhere,
I called your name but my voice was thrown to the winds and
I cried   alone.

I waited for the storm to settle and through the mist I saw
       your face,
I cowered when I saw your eyes – so cold – so faithless and
Hated you for being human.

A thousand years ago I loved you,
A thousand more, I'll still be with you.
■

◄ Sometimes I look at the needle
Full of silver dreams,
Then I think of you, my son, my son.

What future for you
With some-one like me?

I see you through the base of a bottle,
I feel your anger, your hate –
Yet you love me.

If we could be honest with each other,
Perhaps we could say how much we are hurting.
We don't have much choice, do we, my love?
■

◄ Shadows

They pass by in trains
Crouched earnestly behind newspapers,
They sit gravely in buses,
They walk without purpose,
They run if necessary.
They sleep with their wives –
If they can't find another,
They flatter the rich
And ignore the poor.
They trample down the sensitive
And hurt the defenceless,
They sneer at the derelict
Yet offer nothing but smug contempt,
To the desperate, they'll give the final push
To an endless eternity,
But never care to
Hold out a saving hand to the
Lonely.

They pass by in trains
Crouched earnestly behind newspapers,
They sit gravely in buses,
They live. . .
       They die . . .
          They don't give a damn!

■

◄ Memories Of Christmas

It's 4 pm the day before Christmas and I think of you,
I laugh when I remember you said that Christmas was for
    children –
I cried because I never was a child.
I see a tree, all pretty in lights and tinsel,
I see the reflections of the lights in my children's eyes as they
    dance around with joyful anticipation.

I wonder what it is like to be a child,
Would my memories be happy instead of nothing?
Will my children remember being children?

It's Christmas morning,
I hear squeals of delight,
I am woken from a restless sleep with two pairs of arms
    around me,
I feel needed,
God, how I love my children!

I try to feel Christmas through them but, inside, I'm crying,
A nun arrives with a box of food and I feel sick and
    inadequate,
She knows how I feel. (Just put the box down, I say.)

It's Christmas night,
I am exhausted,
I am loved.
■

GERRY BOSTOCK

◀ Gerry Bostock was born in Grafton, New South Wales in 1942. He is of the Bandjalong tribe. Gerry spent his early childhood in the Tweed River area along the Queensland and New South Wales border. He attended a number of schools intermittently in southern Queensland.

Working in unskilled seasonal work such as cotton picking and fruit picking at subsistence level wages and sharing the hardships common in those areas, he obtained a job as a 'dry cleaner'. Possibly his first introduction to mothballs and fashionable clothes. Despite the changes a steady job offered, however, Gerry and his family never forgot nor left in hardship the poorest of the poor of Aboriginal families. He wrote his songs and poetry and in 1961 joined the Australian Army. In 1965 and '67 he toured south-east Asia with the army which he finally left in 1970, unable to reconcile the wearing of a uniform for justice and defence of human rights and dignity with the continual fact of oppression and denial of those very rights to Blacks in Australia.

In 1971, he became directly involved in the struggle for Aboriginal recognition and Land Rights, joining with his well known and widely respected brother, Lester Bostock, in the Black Moratorium and demonstrations for Land Rights. He gave his support to the Aboriginal patriots and the brave, ragged little green tent they erected outside Parliament House, Canberra – the Aboriginal Embassy – in 1972. In that same year, with international focus on Australia through the Aboriginal Embassy, Gerry became a member of the first Australian delegation to visit the People's Republic of China.

After his return from overseas, he began studies at the Open Program of the Australian Television School, becoming production assistant on *Threshold*, a film directed by David Roberts. Since that time he has produced video-tapes, a play *Here Comes The Nigger*, numerous poems and he was production assistant for *The Land My Mother* made by Film Australia.

◄ Childhood Revisited

Oh, to be a child again.

Oh, to relive those same fantasies and childhood dreams
Of heroes and dragons and fairies and witches;
Of good guys fighting bad guys and always winning;
Of stealthily crawling through long grass
Toward an unsuspecting and imaginary foe;
Of lying on my stomach in the back-yard of my father's house
Observing ants and beetles and other insects,
Pretending that they were savage jungle animals
And I was a great hunter in search of my prey;
Or to simply lie on my back in lush, green grass
Watching windswept clouds form different shapes in the blue
    sky.

Oh, to be a child again.

To sit by an open window at night
Watching the sparkling stars changing colour,
And marvel at their beauty;
To learn to say my prayers again,
And again wonder why;
Or to pretend to be asleep
When mum or dad peeped into the room,
And then, after they'd gone,
Pull the sheet over my head and giggle at the joke I'd played;
To again see my parents cry
And want so much to help and protect them,
But not know how.

Oh, to be a child again.

We have forgotten so much in this Age of Technology:
This age of man's journey to the moon and rockets to Mars;
Of great advances in science and medicine;
Of rich mineral discoveries and land exploitation;
And of wars that should shame all mankind.

Oh, to be a child again.

To be pure and unadulterated:
Before having my mind polluted
By the prejudiced thoughts of adults,
And their teachings of the differences in race and colour;
Before learning how to capitalize
On human weaknesses and frailties.

Oh, to be a child again.

■

◄ Night Marauders

A campfire emits an embered glow
And soft sea-breezes gently blow
In the cool of a north Australian night,
Where lies a sleeping Black village – calm and quiet.

The scene is peaceful, sedate and serene.
There's no threat of danger or doom foreseen.
Then, all at once with a shrieking yell
Come night marauders
Like fiendish demons from hell.

Into the village they come at the run
Armed with the shackle and the upraised gun.
On they rush like a human sea
Shooting and killing and laughing with glee.

The blacks grab their babies
And try to take flight
But are subdued and shackled
By the fiends of the night,
Then dragged by their chains to the village compound
While their houses are burned – burned to the ground.

Black women are wailing,
Their children are crying,
Their men are bound helpless
As the village is slowly dying.

■

◄ Uranium

Platinum pens and Yellow Cake
Do not, a proud people make.

■

SELWYN HUGHES _____

Selwyn Hughes is a young, shy man with a quiet intensity and a remarkable aptitude for telling people very little of his life story. I first met him when he was studying with the Aboriginal Task Force, an educational facility especially developed for young Aborigines to train them in basic tertiary studies and community development. Selwyn 'graduated' from the Task Force, and is now somewhere working with Aboriginal people. It is surprising how well the Task Force succeeded, for its former students are now in key positions of administration, community development and on educational committees throughout the Northern Territory, South Australia and Western Australia.

Selwyn Hughes has been published in many community magazines as well as in *Identity* and, one day, we'll see his novels which he intends to keep working on and which draw on the traditional oral history, coming from grass-roots' experience.

◂ # Home On Palm

All my people who are still at home
Still at home on Palm
Don't ever let them put you down
Or try to bring you harm

They are out to justify
Justify they're sane
Then they'll try to rock your boat
So you can take their blame

I don't mean we are Mr Clean
Or Mrs Clean, oh no
I'm damn fed up with the blows
Those scorn that with us grows

A brother of yours has took his stand
For no longer he's sick with shame
Come on let's shoot this old image down
Let's push away our pain

■

◄ Got No Shame

Bludging off the old man
Ain't you got no shame
He's trying to fill the binjies*
As you in past the same

When you was just a young man
Too young to understand
Now give the rest a fair go
You call yourself a man

You drank to boost your manhood
When you were with your friends
Now don't you disappoint them
Prove it to the end

Now you are to their moulding
You find your own way out
Why come back to the old man
To see your kin without

*binjies = bellies
■

LIONEL FOGARTY

◄   Lionel Fogarty was born on Cherbourg Aboriginal Reserve, Queensland. Primary school education on the reserve consisted of counting your money, not reading too well past the 'Don't Trespass' and 'Keep Off' signs level, and not being taught to write 'too well' in case the pupil learnt to write history, or more alarmingly, make written complaint against the abuse of human rights by the authorities and police that occurred daily in the Cherbourg area.

Lionel, always outspoken when his rights were infringed, left Cherbourg for Brisbane where he started speaking publicly about the injustices then occurring, and it was at that time that he joined the Black Housing Service as a field officer. He was a member of the Black Resource Centre Collective from 1975 to 1980, began writing articles, speaking on Aboriginal issues at high schools and universities, and began teaching at the Black Community School, Brisbane. In 1976, he travelled to the U.S.A., and addressed a meeting of the American Indian Treaty Council. In 1979, he wrote *Kargun*, his first book of poetry. It was this book of poems that gave Lionel Fogarty a reputation among the Aboriginal poets. Coming from a tradition of oral poetry, having been forced by assimilationist policy of the government to forego traditional language and to adopt the European tongue, Lionel used the written English like a dervish wields a club.

This was followed in 1982 with *Yoogum Yoogum*, launched at the Commonwealth Writers' Conference held concurrently with the Commonwealth Games in Brisbane. In 1983, his third book of poems, *Kudjela*, was published, and he has worked with Cheryl Buchanan to publish *Murrie Coo-ee*, a collection of poets launched at Koorie Kollij, Victoria. His latest book is *Ngutjl*.

The Worker Who, The Human Who, The Abo Who

Hardware formed relationship from just creating
Our supplier depended for more computer network
knocking miners matters nationally
defensive, came batons modelling awareness
yet securing conspiracy guilty.
Adjourned. tournaments costs considerable obstruction
among its flock.
Fucking and ducking continues
the rugged striking rejects.
beneficial vegetation survives
crippling the market
form their prices
boycott freehold response
operation unfinished
their minds.

We saw shaking hand deal
with an empty chair
strictest supervision
an energetic supervisor dies
senior applicant applies
the media, press
dispute.
Representative accompanied the other
preaching a calmer proposal
then on T.V. millions went conservative
a rolling tribute to the impressive performance
that he gave.

Then the day
the qualitative course
workers went wild.
Strange eyebrows shoot reliable sisters and brothers
whose life is filled
the average hungry man don't vote
the annual implementation of parliament offices
Canberra.
Middle investors partnerships of unity
tease cash
shortfall repayments
compared to humans
$200 million halts business
to developers
so we push metal tinned rationalisation of history.

Bulking health, chalked up
your groups must approve
crossed construction of Aboriginals
reorganising to liquidate our solidarity.

Ask banks to guarantee internally
natural lighting of the moon
Occupied apartheid is only real when remains
are revealed, skeletons.
Your families are soon compelled
to consult about children's rights
who are about to take free integrity in flight.
Committed to preservation of our existence.
Unwillingness.

Pamphlets
Bad pamphlets about what you think is correct
Compensating racist new comers.
Incredible
socially destroyed
powerless
due to do away the people.
produced stores, churches, forestry,
wealthy landowners,
like all humans
must they do
or prevent wars . . . oh oh.

In our quest for living
as an entity
we belong to messages
we belong to the day to day realities
later
much later
additional funds
made the workers have a lot more fun.
Delegates of bodies
advising arrangements
was real real easy.

Our names
cultural
no role
our published papers
ended up in pubs and in bins.
It seems so easy for the computerised idiots
non thinking servants of the robot world
to tick away our lives
with their poison pens
but we will always be
THE WORKER WHO, THE HUMAN WHO, THE ABO WHO
                                                   S
                                                   U
                                                   R
                                                   V
                                                   I
                                                   V
                                                   E
                                                   D

■

Shields Strong, Nulla Nullas Alive

Morning dawning stems that core
won't adore poor poor songs
potentially people quit easy
rarely having arts
personal solos move.
Stunning outrageous woomeras
flew spears that side cornered
Arnhem Lands
Clapsticks local long maybe
normal entrance
finger nail giving painting
sane once again.
Carvings came flying through didgeridoos
over Kimberley roots.
Timber prides
simple ornament like mulga wood crafted
Maningrida distinct types.
Finely grained boomerangs
miniatures proved adults
shaped and thrown in the desert life.
Weaving fabrics
entirely rich relaxed music
designs your ochre coiled of unique colours.
Landscapes
lovers relate
snakes, wild dingo, emus, birds, animals
just like fruit salad.
Traditional authentic coolamons
Yes makers earlier include all.
Fantastic lush property
pumped to a gallon of manure
could you believe that this we were told
was better than
what we had.

An intact society based on quality of life.
How sad for you.
Or shields are strong
Nulla nullas alive.

■

◄ Ecology

I am a frill necked lizard
    roaming, providing
I am refuge by king brown taipan
    highly delightful sea bird
        catches the flint of my star skin colour.

I
Am we pelicans of woodland brolga
    traditional yamming
yes roots, nuts
    differ to geese, hawks, quails
        that number plentiful.

Still I am dugong,
    kangaroo, cockatoo and grasshopper too.
Yes I am a termite, better still
    butterflies are my beetles, wasps friends
You are natures crocodile
    even pythons are not inadequate, nor geckoes.
We are goannas
    after salt water got grounded.

I am death
    harmless.
You are tropic cycles
    swamps got bad affinity
        says who.

Now a dingo arrives
    that diet attractive a woof woof
later bush tucker
    need a barramundi.

Later I am digging sticks
    then I am seeds winnowed for damper
I am club, woomera,
    an agile well-balanced bandicoot
flying fox and an ABORIGINAL
    our systems woven from an eco-system
so don't send us to pollution
    we are just trying to picture
        this life without frustration.

■

ERROL WEST

◀ Errol West was born in Launceston, Tasmania on 20.6.1947. His traditional lineage is the Emeratta tribe of Northern Tasmania. His spirit to be was created on the islands of his ancestors who were annihilated and the remaining descendants were dispossessed in the Bass Strait area.

Errol received only five years of formal education, and that in numerous schools on the islands and mainland of Tasmania. He accompanied his mother and father as they followed the cycle of seasonal work open to Aborigines in the late forties and early fifties. With the support and constant encouragement of his family, he re-entered education and studied to be a primary school teacher.

Errol is presently Chairman of the National Aboriginal Education Committee – the Commonwealth Government's principal policy advisor on issues regarding Aboriginal and Torres Strait Islander education. He was the inaugural Deputy Chairman of this Committee.

◄ There is no one to teach me the songs that bring the Moon
        Bird, the fish or any other thing that makes me what
        I am.

No old women to mend my spirit by preaching my culture to
        me –
No old man with the knowledge to paint my being.
The spectre of the past is what dwells within –
I search my memory of early days to try to make my presence
        real, significant, whole.

I use my childhood memories of places, people and words to
        re-create my identity.
Uncle Leedham, a fine black man is my fondest memory –
He could sing, he could dance and play the mouth organ or
        gum leaf.

His broad shoulders carried me and, as I remember, I found it
        a great pleasure.
I owe him and his contemporaries a debt – and I'll pay –
But there is no one to teach me the songs that bring the
        Moon Bird, the fish or any other thing that makes me
        what I am.

Like dust blown across the plain are the people of the Moon
        Bird –
Whitey said, 'You'll be better over there, you will grow
        again!'
Oh, how wrong he was – why the graves of children run four
        deep – all victims of a foreign disease.
They had no resistance to the legacy of the white invasion –
        or so they must have thought
I am their legacy and I'll not disgrace them,

But there is no one to teach me the songs that bring the
        Moon Bird, the fish or any other thing that makes me
        what I am.

Inside, a warrior of ages rises up – my soul he possesses, his
    righteous indignation is the cup from which I drink –
I do not want blood – just opportunity – to be.

But even with him within there is no one to teach me the
    songs that bring the Moon Bird, the fish or any other
    thing that makes me what I am.

Though wretched the invaders were – for me they created a
    greater wretchedness for they, at least, spoke their
    language, understood their role, yet it was nothing to be
    sought.

My great-grandparents knew their culture and it could not be
    taken from them,
Through the minutes since their life it was taken from me –
    though my warrior within says differently –

Even yet there is no one to teach me the songs that bring the
    Moon Bird, the fish or any other thing that makes me
    what I am.

■

◄ "Please mista do'n take me chilen, please mista do'n"
These words echo through the channels of my heart and
    mind,
A black mother as rich as Croeses in love and loyalty doesn't
    meet the welfare's gait – why, I believe she has become
    too sad to hate what has been and too sick of heart to
    face the future.

The devastation visited on the Aborigine is the holocaust of
    the explosion of the nuclear family – in our people, the
    family goes on and on – it is as endless as we are.

A white man's view is finite, all things here have a beginning,
    and *they* produce the end
Above all things their major intention is to 'assimilate' our
.   people – if the plaintive cry "please mista do'n take me
    chilen, please, mista do'n" is but the beginning
What horrors are at the end.

White man why are you threatened by the Aborigine?
Do you still hear that cry?

"Bring im along nar missus, bring im along"
I hear these words as if spoken to me – NO
I will not be parted from my chilen – my body born them
My love make them grow
My spirit need them
And they need me
Aboriginal man maybe don't have nothing
or so you say
but I as rich as Rockefella
While I got these little ones
"I tink ya know ut too"

You say we cannot mind our children –
you have better things –
I say "my fadda 'e
look afta me an 'e got nuthin" –
I can too.

■

◄ White man's vision
Koories' nightmare, what do you know
you're not there!

Feel the earth; you touch my flesh!
Its only meaning in your quest is the
acquisition of a dollar, white man's vision
Koories' nightmare, what do you know
you're not there!

Aboriginal children, black and white
are the victims of our fight 'culture, culture'
Where is your shadow?
You cleave my heart, my bone, its marrow,
White man's vision, Koories' nightmare,
What do you know
You're not there!

The blood of ages runs in my veins
Yes, my family knows the pains of cultural
devastation, just imagine – devastated by a
wormwood culture – yes your major society is the catalyst;
the vulture.

Lots of drunks and hunger too
I wonder what it means to you –
you're responsible for its presence perpetrated
at a pace which is designed to eliminate my race.
White man's vision, Koories' nightmare,
What do you know
You're not there!

Kids with dirty noses know the effect of the catalyst –
Even their appearance faces your condemnation,
These kids see their hollow future –
No, they are not the fatalists,
White man's vision,
Koories' nightmare
What do you know
You're not there!

■

◄ Misty mountains tell me the secrets you hold, of men
and women, the young and the old who graced your treed
slopes and from your sweet water streams drank to their
content. Are their spirits still occupying your beautiful form
as totemic beings ensuring your continued existence.

The Banjil soars high, surveying his possession, his eye as
clear as your sweet water and his body as firm as your mature
gum nut and cumbungi root, yet is his eye responsive to their
physical absence? Does he, also the hunted, long to see the
campfire's smoke, long to hear the songs and the voices of
both your aged and your little ones?

These mountains are lonely for their tread in both stealth
and joy to give up that which makes its heart beat for their
pleasure, their comfort, their presence, is her greatest gift.

As a grandmother who has seen successive generations from
her children's children, so has the mountain long time, loved
her children's children – but they are no more in visible
evidence to comfort her. Does she as a grandmother of ages
close her eyes and enjoy the living memory of her lifeline,
children whose stories and dances and songs made her heart
swell with absolute contentment.

In their absence, white men have occupied her pulsing breast,
not content with her natural beauty they have engaged in
rude plastic surgery on your most gracious nature; they have
divested you, in this they have scarred your silken
appearance. I watch the mists begin to dissipate as the sun's
rays bear down on your gentle crown, I touch the leaves,
flowers and the grass. They seem to be suddenly deluged with
droplets of water – can I convince myself they are not your
tears.

■

Sitting, wondering, do I have a place here?
The breast of Mother Earth bore me, yet long I host a shell of
emptiness, a human husk winnowed in the draught of history,
    my
essence ground on the mill of white determination.

I fight though mortally wounded, life blood and spirit ebbing
    away
in the backwater of despair, caused by long-winded
    politicians'
promises and administration's cumbersome gait;
another realisation of my hopelessness produces; another
    promise,
implementation of a band-aid gimmick, you had better hurry
    it's
getting late, red tape, budgets, strategies,
Rape!

Return me to my beloved land, let me be me, don't you
    understand?
All I want is a private dying in the arms of my Mother earth,
    she
too is suffering; as a mother must when her children are
    ripped
away from her love, and the safety of her arms, no more to be
    cradled,
tenderly caressed by her heavenly smoldering essence.

The Gubba-ment don't try its best, it really does reflect the
    spirit of the majority
While my body is complying, my spirit has unrest and decays,
it does not matter what you say
all you do is 'smooth the dying pillow' an act which is
    constituted
of ignorance, hatred, or worse disinterest.

I long for my Mother Earth, though her graggy face has been
    altered by
concrete paths, her beautiful complexion pockmarked,
    scarred, ruined
by white man's highways, her enchanting brown eyes are
    glazed by
monolithic cataracts which reach to the sky. Yet for all her
    arid
beauty I ache for her embrace.

■

◀ I feel the texture of her complexion with both hand and
        heart;
    I shut my eyes; still I cannot divorce the loving memory of
        her touch, her influence on my life.

To separate from my only reality is impossible, as long as I
        live – is that not a fatalist's view considering her future?
    Mining, digging, drilling, a cancer attacking the essence of my
        life; in unity our spirits scream Stop! Desist!
    We can bear no more your attack.

Under better law this assault could not occur –
    my brothers and sisters would stand, a human wall, a barrier
        against this vicious attack – yet now, with almost none to
        defend her you rip out her heart, her spleen and liver –
        mining, digging, drilling, a cancer attacking the essence
        of my life.

You destroy her lovely face and scar her gentle body – as we
        can see; to your disgrace – I shut my eyes; still I cannot
        divorce the loving memory of her touch, her influence on
        my life –

Songs of another time, were sung – and so she had remained
        – I know not those songs or the singers to face yet with
        them I am entwined –
    There are the songs anew, the answer in them lies, I take
        nothing for myself, I wish to nourish and nurture – see
        she grows in strength.

∎

JIM CARLSON

◄   Jim Carlson was reared in a weatherboard shack in the bush on the outskirts of Kiama, New South Wales.

His mother was from the local tribe. His father was of English and Norwegian descent, and worked the fishing trawlers and as a casual labourer. He encouraged Jim and his younger brother to study their own culture as well as his.

Jim attended Kiama Public School, leaving when he turned fifteen years of age. He moved shortly afterwards to Port Kembla where he lived with his uncle and aunt on the 'mission'. He lived there for a number of years, moving to Berkeley to find work on the waterboard.

It was in Berkeley that he met his wife Noeleene on a 'blind date'. They subsequently married and are still together after eighteen years, of which Jim says 'We're solidly happy and proud parents of seven wonderful kids, four girls and three boys and we're rearing two others, my wife's young brother and our nephew.'

He and his wife were involved in helping set up the Illawarra Aboriginal Corporation in Wollongong, of which he was the chairman for some time. He has just completed the Aboriginal University Preparation Course and, 'I hope to help my people by going on to Uni. and studying law or creative arts or history, and keep on writing poetry.'

■

◄ I need appreciation
and plenty of guts
to do what I want
'cause I know that I must.

I must help my people
regain *ALL* their land
to help their survival
as much as I can.

The children, the parents
and all of their kin
to help all our Nation
get together *AGAIN*!

■

◄ Stand up, be proud,
Let 'em know you're black,
You feel it when your heart beats,
Don't fear their attacks!

You know that your nation
Will always be here,
Don't worry, white fella
You came, we don't care.

You gave us education,
Now that's the way
We'll fight you, we'll beat you,
We'll do it –
            one day!

■

BERYL PHILP-CARMICHAEL YUNGHA-DHU

◄   Beryl Philp-Carmichael, Yungha-dhu, was born on 2.7.1935 on Old Menindee 'Mission', New South Wales. She is of the Ngyampa tribe.

Beryl spent her early life on the Old Menindee Mission, being delivered at birth with the help of a tribal woman and her *Nghulli*, spirit totem the emu. Educated by her old people in traditional bush survival she also attended the mission school, attaining sixth class primary before leaving school at age twelve.

Moving around with her family and the old people as they worked at jobs such as droving, burr-cutting, rabbiting and fencing, as wood cutters and as stockmen, she absorbed the spiritual levels of our old culture, and the newer, leaner complexities of communication in a written language devoid of the depth and conciseness of the mnemonic oral structure. Most of Beryl's life was spent on stations in the top end of New South Wales until 1966 when the family moved to Menindee township to give their children a better chance of education. (She has ten children in all.) She became active in Aboriginal community affairs and education and the struggles of our people to effectively bring about change. With the history of the 'mission days' embedded in her mind and, recognising the need to document that history for the sake of furthering the children's education, she began writing stories and poems. She also became President of the Mothers' Club, President of the Parents' and Citizens' Committee, a member of the Aboriginal Education Consultative Group in Western N.S.W., and Community Schools' Liaison Officer in the Broken Hill area. In spite of these commitments she still found time to produce a book of poems and stories, called *Mayagarthi*, obtainable from Black Books, Tranby College, Glebe, N.S.W.

◄ Dust Storm

Old man kicking up dust –
    Emu's close by –
        Old man waving red rag,
            Emu opens his eyes.

Old man moving faster,
    Dust swirling mad and high –
        Emu's senses tells him be cautious
            As old man and weapon close by.

Hunting Emu can be fun
    And played for hours –
        Only trouble is dust storm –
            Bringing on showers.

Old man moves for cover,
    Cliff is overhanging –
        Old man wait in comfort –
            Cliff blocks out the sun.

■

◄ Pemulwy – A Visitation

Poor Pemulwy
    we never met?
    (not in this life)
some say you're asleep/not living
gone to England   to see
    the kings/and/queens/and them
your fire buried with that other fella
    King Arthur
    who
    fought for his people
    their ways   their dignity!
Rich Pemulwy
    we always meet
across oceans of despair
through the magic fires of our hearts.
  ■

◄ Mother

To have you at home when all have gone,
    To hear your voice – I'm never alone,
Your hair of silver shining bright,
    Your worktorn hands still hold me tight –
Your smile of welcome at the door –
    The crust of bread you gave the poor . . .
I add them up – what do I see?
    A lovely lady pouring tea
With steady hands of ribboned steel,
    Her furrowed brow all wrinkled marked,
Her love for all is readily sparked,
    Guiding our steps as she knew how
With tender fingertips soothing our brow . . .
    Do not forsake her – this lady of old,
As she is the mother we must uphold.
  ■

◄ My Dad

When we were in trouble –
    You were around,
When afraid of the dark –
    You were around,
When sickness overcame us –
    You were around.
On rough, stormy nights –
    You were around.

You gave us your all –
    When you were around
Nothing frightened us –
    When you were around,
Aches, pains, fears disappeared
    When you were around
Battling alone without you
    Gets hard at times –
But the love and beliefs
    You bestowed upon us
Is among the great gifts
    Of all mankind.

■

ELIZABETH BROWN

◄ Elizabeth Brown's birthright is Caiwarra on the Paroo River, Budjara people country. As a child she lived on stations in outback Queensland with her sister and brothers. She was sent to a hostel for schooling, then moved to the city, where she finished school. These poems were written at the age of 18 years. Since writing them she has travelled over a lot of Australia, living in bush and town Aboriginal communities. Her wish is to return to her grandmother's country.

◄ You Got
You Got To Be Told

Driving to work, planned day ahead
stop at the light changing to red
cars accelerate, time in flight
passing the present, at a green light.

Ride the lift, to the system
hours to go, hours gone past
end of the day, hang up that mask
the company pays, at the end of the week
times up number, go home to sleep.

Moving along, crowded roads
individuals carry, heavy loads
Traffic stops:
Signal the paperboy walking near
time to be told what to fear.

Paper smells of money greed
the world at war, life the seed
shot to death, indecision
news printed, mountains risen
people, poverty, capitalists drool
the colours change
Traffic lights rule.

■

◄ Spiritual Land

A distant rock, a far off land
deeply planted stands
loyal and grand.
Remembrance of timeless years gone by
alone at night, the rock will cry.

Hunger for money, stripped the land
mined the Earth in which she's bound
bulldozed the surface, to graze their beef
distorting the Earth in disbelief.

Soon the wind will change course
swept in fortune, a powerful force
nature reclaims a desolate mess
reclaims the race, who related best.

Peace, strength, remakes a home
a land once more
free to roam.

■

KEVIN GILBERT
WIRADJURI _____

◄   I was born on the banks of the Lachlan (Kalara) River at
Condobolin on 10th July 1933. I am the youngest of eight
children born to Jack Gilbert and Rachel Naden. From the early
1930s and up to the mid 1950s, I was on the receiving end of
White Australia's apartheid system. We were not allowed to be in
'town' later than 30 minutes after the last movie was over. We
were separated from the white audience by a roped enclosure,
not allowed into hospital dormitories, but kept out on the
verandahs of the hospital known as the 'boong' ward where
pillows, sheets, bedding were stencilled in black with the word
'Abo' on them.

Up until the 1950s, there were no pensions or social service
payments. Blacks were not counted on the census. When we
visited 'missions' where our relatives lived we had to have a
'pass' from the manager, or, if he was in a bad mood, we were
kept away from family.

Children were removed forcibly from mothers and pet dogs
shot in target practice by police. Some Blacks were not allowed
any closer than ten miles of the township where whites lived, and
where, even after the war, I saw my brothers who had served in
the second world war as enlisted men, hunted like felons from the
bar of the pub where they asked for a beer.

So, I was born Black. Black and honest in a white society that
spoke oh so easily of 'justice', 'democracy', 'fair go', 'christian
love', and had me and mine living in old tin sheds, under scraps of
iron, starving on what we could catch – goanna, rabbit, kangaroo,
or on what we could find – bread and fat, treasures of old lino and
hessian bags from the white man's rubbish tip to keep us a little
bit dry and warmer in the winter.

Orphaned when I was seven years old, I was left in the care of
my elder sisters (my brothers had joined the army). I went to first
class primary in Leeton where I was soon embroiled in con-
tinuous attacks by hordes of white children, and, having learnt
well the appropriate response to attack, angry parents were soon

calling on the police and teachers to 'do' something. I and my two younger sisters were sent to the orphanages in Sydney.

Returning to Wiradjuri country at the age of eleven, thanks to my sister Joyce who married a soldier and had turned seventeen, I went to live in the tents and under 'roof' of flattened square kerosene tins and hessian. Picking grapes, getting wet in the house every time it rained, having no 'kitchen' or water-taps, or electric light, not even a wooden floor, I came to believe more in the truth my Uncles and Aunts taught me. Old Uncle Burrawang, the last of the cicatriced men, my old uncles, friends like the Bloomfields, the Carberries, the Ingrams, the Coes, the Simpsons, the Dargins, Monighans, Quales, Bambletts, the Williams, the Goolagongs, Lords, Murrays, Melrose, my old Princess Subina were my reality, my people. With all the rags, little tucker, few blankets, ours was a greater love, greater truth and being, a greater spirituality than any one of the white Christians had ever possessed. Family names ring along the Darling, the Murrumbidgee, the Lachlan; a great black tentacle of home stretching right through to wherever the tribes met. So I was born Black and our truth was the truest truth of all.

Educated to fifth class primary, I left school and became a rabbit-trapper, a grape picker, a seasonal worker. To earn a crust, or a fare to a movie, I picked up scraps of copper wire and lead to sell. I gathered empty soft-drink bottles to buy bread, I walked the dusty roads picking up scraps of wool from dead sheep carcases, and tufts of wool clinging to bushes to sell it as 'dead wool' to the skin merchants. I carried rabbit traps in a kids' billy-cart up and down hills where, after setting the traps, I fell asleep exhausted on a hessian bag, to awaken, covered in frost, sniffling from cold, not just because times were hard, but because I was *BLACK* and the white man had taken my country from my people and kept me and my people as victims, as slaves.

In 1957 when I was twenty-three years of age, I received a sentence of penal servitude for life for the murder of my white wife. Of which I can only say that, I was a Black boy in a white court where the jury, the judge, the lawyers were *ALL* white. What chance of justice? Thus I spent fourteen and a half years in prison.

I wrote my first play, *The Cherry Pickers*, based upon the experience of my own people as seasonal workers and their search for spirituality and justice. In 1973 I wrote *Because a White Man'll Never Do It*, a major political work, and in 1978 I wrote *Living Black*, published by Penguin. This book was a collection of oral history and, now in its fifth edition, is used widely as a text book in secondary schools within Australia.

In 1978, Queensland University Press brought out my volume of poetry called *People ARE Legends*.

Today, I am the Chairman of our Aboriginal Sovereign *Treaty '88 Campaign*, which is calling on Australians to acknowledge that this, *OUR* land was not *terra nullius*, unoccupied wasteland as claimed by Captain James Cook and the colonists, but that we, the Aboriginals, have our right to ownership and possession and that approaching the bicentenary, it is time that a properly constituted treaty was entered into. The purpose of all my writings is to present the truth of Aboriginality and justice, for these two great and wonderful principles are the *ONLY* principles upon which this land and its people can survive and build on the values my people knew. It is the only principle upon which this land can ultimately survive.

◄ Tree

I am the tree
the lean hard hungry land
the crow and eagle
sun and moon and sea
I am the sacred clay
which forms the base
the grasses vines and man
I am all things created
I am you and
you are nothing
but through me the tree
you are
and nothing comes to me
except through that one living gateway
to be free
and you are nothing yet
for all creation
earth and God and man
is nothing
until they fuse
and become a total sum of something
together fuse to consciousness of all
and every sacred part aware
alive in true affinity.

■

Kiacatoo

On the banks of the Lachlan they caught us
at a place called Kiacatoo
we gathered by campfires at sunset
when we heard the death-cry of curlew
women gathered the children around them
men reached for their nulla and spear
the curlew again gave the warning
of footsteps of death drawing near
Barjoola whirled high in the firelight
and casting his spear screamed out 'Run!'
his body scorched quickly on embers
knocked down by the shot of a gun
the screaming curlew's piercing whistle
was drowned by the thunder of shot
men women and child fell in mid-flight
and a voice shouted 'We've bagged the lot'
and singly the shots echoed later
to quieten each body that stirred
above the gurgling and bleeding
a nervous man's laugh could be heard
'They're cunning this lot, guard the river'
they shot until all swimmers sank
but they didn't see Djarrmal's family
hide in the lee of the bank
Djarrmal warned 'Stay quiet or perish
they're cutting us down like wild dogs
put reeds in your mouth – underwater
we'll float out of here under logs'
a shot cracked and splintered the timber
the young girl Kalara clutched breath
she later became my great grandma
and told the story of my people's death

The Yoorung bird cries by that place now
no big fish will swim in that hole
my people pass by that place quickly
in fear with quivering soul
at night when the white ones are sleeping
content in their modern day dreams
we hurry past Kiacatoo
where we still hear shuddering screams
you say 'Sing me no songs of past history
let us no further discuss'
but the question remains still unanswered
How can you deny us like Pilate
refusing the rights due to us.
The land is now all allocated
the Crown's common seal is a shroud
to cover the land thefts the murder
but can't silence the dreams of the proud.

▪

Mum

Fifteen dogs prowled
baying tense
unkempt and shaggy
hair and bones
marked out their form
and spoke of lean
and leaner times
at their old home
still faithful yet
as if to say
there's more than food
that makes us stay
a quality we feel and know
to make our very bristles glow
with love from those within
and passing through
the canvas door
I started in surprise
I saw
a woman lying on a bed
legs made of packing cases
dead – she never moved
the yellowed sheet
the tattered bedspread
at her feet
the squalor of the ragged tent
the greasy pots I near gave vent
to screams of outrage horror mind
raced crazily a pounding drum
a man's soft gentle voice 'My Mum
she's blind and seventeen
years of it I've never seen
the rhyme or reason for the act
they won't give us a house
the fact
speaks for itself the tent the bed
the dogs are better off' he said.

'My Mum she's blind she's now asleep
she'll wake up soon
the fact of it
she won't go nowhere
but the bed
Commission said no house
not fit
or Black or something and . . .'
he said
'the dogs live better in this land
and we'd do better dead
my Mum she's blind'
he said.

■

Gularwundul's Wish

The listless dingo whelps – lolled by the door
if door it could be called – four mulga sticks
a tattered old tarpaulin and some bags
propped up with tin served as a house
wall roof and floor in place of iron and brick
the cooking place two granite rocks
three rounded small and well-aged mulga sticks
were glowing white with heat where centres met
one black and well-burnt can called 'billy' in these parts
five black crows scratched at scraps nearby a 'roo bone,
    sinews hewn
from near the thigh for binding of a spear
which proudly sat on show well heeled
upon the powdery sand that blew in constant eddies
whirling high as if to carve
the weathered features of the tribal man before me
weeping from his sand-blight eyes:

'It ain't much I'm asking ain't it?
Runnin' water h'in a tap it's me grand-daughter
saw tap pictures on the Territory tourist map
I asked the welfare fella Department of Affairs
for Aborigines you know. It ain't much ain't it?
I asked him when he came to consult.
'That's good thinkin' Gularwundul' to me he said 'that true
you're not greedy for Toyota big money or a gun
but you just want some water in a tap so it'll run
I'll survey the camps' he told me true
'It's good thoughts for everyone to have clean water
in a tank straight from a tap to run
you'll have it mate tell grand-daughter
her little wish come true and make everyone happy
we'll survey the other camps, the mob, the whole way
    through.'

'It ain't much ain't it but we ain't got it yet
three years passed now we get our water
from the creek and plenty from the "wet".
The grand-daughter she now gits
all the water that she needs
we buried her beside the river where casuarinas bleed
it ain't much ain't it?
If you see that man down south that man Canberra D.A.A.
tell him I don't want it I don't want that water now
forget about that thing survey.'

I gave my word a fragile thing
a vapour from my mouth and held the promise in my mind
when next I travelled south and I saw him
leather chaired and swivelled flat feet falling from the desk
'Have you seen' he said to me 'the new community plan that
        I put in . . .'
expansive was his grin disarming me to tact
when I told him of Gularwundul
he said 'Humbug! It's a fact
they WANT to live the way they do
they want their way to stay – you southern blacks
and do-gooders will never ever learn'
he said in scorn
'and if you don't believe me I'll carry out a wide survey
they want to live the way they do
they don't want it any other way.'

It ain't much to ask for ain't it
to make peoples' dreams come true
when tyrants rule and children die
when every other option's closed
there's one last thing to do . . .
ain't it?

■

Same Old Problem

Remember the hate
the mortality rate
the tumbledown shacks and the rain
the children you bury
the pain that you hide
the despair and denial out-back
you're down and you're beaten
a glimmer of hope
like a sigh on the wind passes by
you cannot explain
but
you're *their* problem again
by your stubborn refusal to die
your water-bag's empty
the Miners jeer by
their Toyota dust burns your throat
November Elections
the issues are Black
there's iron where your God-heart won't bend
remember the rivers of water
your chant
falls dead with the horsemen in sight
you'll 'smell off' the cattle
'you cannot drink here'
your tribesmen go thirsty this night
your tribesmen go thirsting this night.

You look at Pleiades
sisters and snake, the devil-dog dingo a'chase
eternal spirits that light up the sky
then lo – a bright streak mars their face
a satellite whirls where only gods tread
another site to be mined
you try hard to be wise and hold the hate in
shedding rivers of tears for the blind
you bend over the shovel knowing heart-wise the score
some government johnny will sigh
'another one dead take his name off the list
these days they just kark it like flies.'

■

The New True Anthem

Despite what Dorothea has said
about the sun scorched land
you've never really loved her
nor sought to make her grand
you pollute all the rivers
and litter every road
your barbaric graffitti
cut scars where tall trees grow
the beaches and the mountains
are covered with your shame
injustice rules supremely
despite your claims to fame
the mud polluted rivers
are fenced off from the gaze
of travellers and the thirsty
for foreign hooves to graze
a tyranny now rules your soul
to your own image blind
a callousness and uncouth ways
now hallmarks of your kind

Australia oh Australia
you could stand proud and free
we weep in bitter anguish
at your hate and tyranny
the scarred black bodies writhing
humanity locked in chains
land theft and racial murder
you boast on of your gains
in woodchip and uranium
the anguished death you spread
will leave the children of the land
a heritage that's dead

Australia oh Australia
you could stand tall and free
we weep in bitter anguish
at your hate and tyranny.

■

◄ Celebrators '88

The blue-green greyish gum leaves
blew behind the bitter banksia that bent
in supplication silently bereaved
bereft of the black circle that once sat
around its base to stroke and chant the songs
that made the rivers flow and life wax fat
the legends and the river now replaced
by sheep torn gullies and a muddy silt
that sluggishly and sullen in retreat
throws up its mud to signal its defeat
the carking crows had changed their song grown deep
from tasting human flesh that left to reek
beneath the unpolluted sun in pioneer days
now veiled in smog so spirits cannot peek
the river dove grown silent fearing song
will bring the hunter with his thundering death
the kookaburra laughs in disbelief then waits again
in fear with bated breath.

The legislators move their pen in poise
like thieves a'crouch above the pilfered purse
how many thousand million shall they give
to celebrate the Bicentenary
and cloak the murders in hilarity
and sing above the rumble of the hearse.

■

◄ Peace And The Desert

As campfire embers gleam
I hear the call
of curlews singing birth
or death for some
the still night desert air
in trembling
sounds sighs of trespass
at the distant drums
the dawn comes, hushed
primeval night in flight
leaves fluttering the imprint of the sound
of carnage and the carnivores' might
still, still a wren like hope starts warbling
a lizard stirs surviving on a rock
an emu, two seek water from a spring
the eagles focus eagerly their sight
ajoy at what the bloodied night may bring
faint eddies lift and swirl
the sands convulse
to some macabre dance
in dervish glee
smack stingingly upon my cheeks my brow
then screams its fury over this now dead sea.

The sun beams down benign its energy
vibrating molecules to life and birth
magnificent this generous warmth to all
save me, the only creature out of place
homo sapiens the plunderer supreme
come to exploit to ravish rent aside
whatever secret wealth or life remain
generated in this ancient land
and washed ashore by some great ancient tide
the drums beat near
some fellow man perhaps
or army marching to their ritual
to kill what represents the human form
or that which may frustrate their narrow will
peace, peace let there be peace the millions cry
great nations tremble fearfully at threat
their tall flags fly defiantly and bless
their squadrons in their grim green battle-dress.

■

◂ Won't You Dad?

If all the lovely melodies
in all the world were ever sung
and all the masters' masterpieces
in the greatest galleries ever hung
and all the statues David and
the poems and the works of man
were to burn bright for death's delight
throughout our land
a little child looked up and smiled
and beamed with pride and love and joy
and said: 'You won't let them drop that bomb
on me Daddy. You'll stop them, won't you Daddy?'

His question mark
was like an arc all ringed around
with burning flame
I said in loving confidence:
'We'll stop them, child'
but in my heart is fear and burning shame
I actually *PAY* the Man
to make the *BOMB*
I pay him Tax to sing
his song of hate
I keep the war-dog on his chain
I help to feel and feed his hate
I *PAY THE MAN* to make the bomb
to hold the world and my child in fear
I close my heart to human beings
as if afraid
when love draws near

It's *ME* who's wrong
it's *ME* who'll burn the song
it's me who'll burn the lovely melody
because I fear other humans near
who may somehow flood human love to me
the flame will burn and melt the eyes
of my children as they turn
to me and say with love for me
and faith today:
'You will stop them dropping the bomb on me
won't you Dad?'
▪

◄ Taipan

Have you heard how the Taipan
crouches and waits
how it waits for its shadow to fall
the trespasser strides aware in contempt
kicking the reeds where he hides
how he waits with the flick
of his tongue grins a gleam
accepting the challenge of death
how he waits and he waits
with his sibilant breath
and a flick of his tongue
for the test.
▪

INDEX OF FIRST LINES

◀ **W**

◀ **Y**

AUTHOR INDEX

ACKNOWLEDGEMENTS

For permission to reprint the poems in this anthology, acknowledgement is made to the following:

Debby Barben: 'To Look Yet Not Find', 'Four White Walls', 'Eight Beds, Eight Lockers', and 'Do You Know What You're Saying', to the author.

Steve Barney: 'Vision' and 'Black People Cry' to *Murrie-Coo-ee: A collection of Aboriginal writing*, Murrie Coo-ee (1983), to Cheryl Buchanan.

Gerry Bostock: 'Childhood Revisited', 'Night Maurauders' and 'Uranium' from *Black Man Coming* (1980), to the author.

Graham Brady: 'Voice from the bush Through me', from *Murrie Coo-ee: A collection of Aboriginal Writing* (1983), to Cheryl Buchanan.

Elizabeth Brown: 'You Got, You Got To Be Told' and 'Spiritual Land', to the author.

Jim Carlson: 'I need appreciation' and 'Stand up, be proud', to the author.

Iris Clayton: 'River Bidgee', 'The Last Link', 'The Black Rat', and 'Kidnappers', to the author.

Stephen Clayton: 'The Good Old Days', 'Soul Music', 'Boom Time', 'Redfern at Night' and 'Sunshine Prisoner "470"', to the author.

Vicky Davey: 'The Shadow of Life' from *Black Voices*, Victorian Secondary Education Multicultural Project and Ethnic Relations, to the author.

Jack Davis: 'First Born', 'Aboriginal Reserve', 'Slum Dwelling' and 'My Brother, My Sister' from *The First Born and Other Poems* (1983) J. M. Dent, to the author, 'Aboriginal Australia' and 'Urban Aboriginal' from *Jagardoo: Poems from the Aboriginal Australia* (1978) Methuen, to the author.

Ernie Dingo: 'The tracks and the traces', 'Aboriginal achievement' and 'We are not', to the author.

Frank Doolan: 'Who Owns Darling Street?', 'The Last Fullblood', 'The Whiteman Is The Judge', to the author.

Mary Duroux: 'Dirge for a Hidden Art' from *Black Voices*,

Victorian Secondary Education Multicultural Project and Ethnic Relations, to the author; and 'Lament For A Dialect' to the author.

Pam Errinaron Williams: 'Torn Apart', to the author.

Jim Everett: 'Old Co'es', 'Ode To Salted Mutton Birds', 'Rest Our Spiritual Dead' and 'The White Man Problem', to the author.

Lionel Fogarty: 'The Worker Who, The Human Who, The Abo Who', 'Shields Strong, Nulla Nullas Alive' and 'Ecology' from Yoogum Yoogum: Beyond the despair of Aboriginal oppression towards an understanding of total cultural unity (1982), Penguin, to the author.

Kevin Gilbert: 'Same Old Problem' from Poetry Australia, to the author; 'Kiacatoo', 'Mum', 'Gularwundul's Wish', 'New True Anthem', 'Celebrators '88', 'Peace and the Desert', 'Won't You Dad', and 'Taipan', to the author.

Selwyn Hughes: 'Home On Palm' and 'Got No Shame', to the author.

Colin Johnson: 'They Give Jacky Rights', 'Jacky Demonstrates For Land Rights', 'Jacky Hears The Century Cry', 'Jacky Sings His Songs', 'Reincarnation', to the author; other versions published in The Song Circle of Jacky and Selected Poems (1986) Hyland House; 'Streets', to the author.

Eva Johnson: 'A Letter To My Mother' and 'Remember' from Differences; Writings by Women (1985) Waterloo Press, to the author; 'Right To Be' and 'Weevilly Porridge', to the author.

Grandfather Koori: 'Never Blood So Red', 'Massacre Sandhill' and 'The Song In The Symbol', to the author.

Hyllus Maris: 'The Season's Finished' and 'Spiritual Song Of The Aborigines' from Black Voices, Victorian Secondary Education Multicultural Project and Ethnic Relations, to the author.

Rex Marshall: 'Burrel Bullai', 'Buddgelin Bay' and 'Little Brown Jacks — Nyimbung' from Aboriginal Verse, North Coast Institute of Aboriginal Community Education, to the author.

Jenny Hargraves Nampijinpa: 'Yuntalpa-Ku/Child Leave The Tape Recorder', to the author.

Pansy Rose Napaljarri: 'Marlu-Kurlu/The Kangaroo' and Muturna-Jarra-Kurlu Kujalpa-Pala Wangkaja/Two women sit in the shade away from the hot sun', to the author.

Valerie Patterson Napanaṅka: 'Ṅapa-Kurlu/The Rain' and 'Nantuwu-Kurlu/The Horse', to the author.

Irene James Napurrurla: 'Ṅapa-Kurlu/The Water', to the author.

Rhonda Samuel Napurrurla: 'Ṅati-Nyanu-Jarra-Kurlu/The Two Mothers', to the author.

Dyan Newson: 'Crowther-Ours' and 'Turnabouts', to the author.

Oodgeroo Noonuccal (Kath Walker): 'Colour Bar', 'Gooboora, the Silent Pool' and 'The Unhappy Race' from *We Are Coming* (1964) Jacaranda Press; 'Municipal Gum' from *The Dawn is at Hand* (1966) Jacaranda Press; these and 'The Past' and 'Time is Running Out' from *My People*, (1970) Jacaranda Press, to the author.

Julie Watson Nungarrayi: 'Yapa Kujalpalu Nyinaja Nyurruwiyi/ Sorry', to the author.

Charmaine Papertalk-Green: 'Wanna be White' from *The Penguin Book of Australian Women Poets* (1986) Penguin, to the author; 'Have You Starved?', 'Pension Day', 'No One To Guide Us', to the author.

Beryl Philp-Carmichael: 'Dust Storms', 'Pemulwy – A Visitation', 'Mother', 'My Dad' from *Mayagarthi* (1986) Yungha-dhu Press, to the author.

Luke Roma: 'I picture your face', 'I drink your love' and 'Vision' from *Murrie Coo-ee: A collection of Aboriginal Writing* (1983), to Cheryl Buchanan.

W. Les Russell: 'God Gave Us Trees To Cut Down' in *Greed for Green*, Impact Media Productions, to the author; 'Tarli Karng: Twilight Snake' from *This Australia*, Winter 1985 vol. 4, no. 3, to the author; 'Red', 'Ngarnbarndtar', 'The Developers', 'Nuclear Winter', to the author.

Bobbi Sykes: 'Requiem', 'Fallin'', 'One Day', 'Rachel', 'Final Count', 'Cycle' from *Love Poems and Other Revolutionary Actions*, Saturday Centre, to the author; 'Prayer To The Spirit Of The New Year', to the author.

Daisy Utemorrah: 'Mary's Plea' from '*Identity*' and *Black Voices*, Victorian Secondary Education Multicultural Project and Ethnic Relations, to the author.

Robert Walker: 'Life is Life', 'Solitary Confinement', 'Unreceived Messages' and 'Okay, Let's Be Honest' from *Up! Not Down Mate* (1981) Catholic Chaplaincy to Aborigines, to Charlotte Szekely.

Maureen Watson: 'Black Child' *Meanjin* (1977) vol. 36, no. 4, to the author; 'Stepping Out', 'Female of the Species', 'Memo to JC', to the author.

Archie Weller: 'Untitled Series', to the author.

Laury Wells: 'Distress Upon the Farm', 'The Nomads', 'Prelude' and 'The "Sorcerer"', to the author.

Errol West: 'There is no one to teach me the songs that bring the Moon Bird' from *Pride Against Prejudice: Reminiscences of a Tasmanian Aborigine* (1984) Australian Institute of Aboriginal Studies, to the author; '"Please mista do'n take me chilen, please mista do'n"', 'White Man's Vision', 'Misty mountains tell me the secrets you hold, of men', 'I feel the texture of her complexion with both hand and heart', 'Sitting wondering, do I have a place here?', to the author.

Joy Williams: 'Rachel', 'A thousand years ago I loved you', 'Sometimes I look at the needle', 'Shadows' and 'Memories of Christmas', to the author.

Every effort has been made to trace copyright holders, but in a few cases this has proved impossible. The publishers would be interested to hear from any copyright holders not acknowledged here or acknowledged incorrectly.

FOR THE BEST IN PAPERBACKS, LOOK FOR THE

PENGUIN

Dreamtime Nightmares Bill Rosser

The early settlers in Northern Australia, building their extensive stations, were short of labour – until they discovered the ability of the Aboriginal men and women as stockriders.

'There is Jack Punch, who in the wink of an eye could revert to his tribal life-style, if given the chance . . . Harry Spencer did not know the white man's word until he was a man. Poor Harry! When he first saw sheep he thought they were Shetland ponies . . . 'Peggy James and Dorothy Webster are two tribal women in dresses and shoes. Usually laconic, it is only when they talk about the "old times" that their fat cheeks crease with a smile, even though "Those times was bloody crook mate."

It is Bill Rosser's unique talent of setting the scene and then teasing out the life stories of fellow Aboriginal women and men which makes *Dreamtime Nightmares* such a compelling book.

Living Black   Blacks Talk to Kevin Gilbert

National Book Council Award for Australian Literature, 1978

'Aboriginal Australia underwent a rape of the soul so profound that the blight continues in the minds of most blacks today.'

Kevin Gilbert has talked with his people and taped their story – in the bush, in small country towns, and in the black ghettos of Sydney and Melbourne.

'What emerges is a damning indictment of the white man for his despicable discrimination, his injustice and intolerance, his ignorance and, above all, his failure to recognize the Aboriginal as a fellow human being – a human being with a deep sense of pride, a history as old as time and an affinity with his land that the white man will never understand.'

Herald

'A frank and compelling social document which exposes themes and issues important in the everyday lives of Aboriginal Australians. Its criticisms and lessons should not be ignored.'

Neville Perkins
Australian